A Corpse and a Cat

by

Rena Leith

*A Cass Peake Cozy Mystery,
Book Four*

A Corpse and a Cat

Cover Art by *Debbie Taylor*

The Wild Rose Press, Inc.
PO Box 708
Adams Basin, NY 14410-0708
Visit us at www.thewildrosepress.com

Publishing History
First Edition, 2024
Trade Paperback ISBN 978-1-5092-5831-4
Digital ISBN 978-1-5092-5832-1

A Cass Peake Cozy Mystery, Book Four
Published in the United States of America

Dedication

For Emma and Max

Other Books By Rena Leith

A Corpse for Christmas
Coastal Corpse
Murder Beach
The Great Christmas Jelly Cookie Hunt

Prologue

Thoris found the body quite by accident. The dead thing lay there quiescent on the beach on the far side of the observatory. She might have missed it altogether, but as they meandered around the base of the building, the moon slid out from behind a cloud and shone down on the fish-belly white skin that gleamed dully in its nakedness.

Doris steered Thor's body over for a closer look. Thor really was a very intelligent cat as cats go, but he was a very big, very lazy black beast. When Doris inhabited him to leave the precincts of Cass' beach bungalow, she had to make a special effort, as Thoris—the possession—to move Thor along to where she wanted him to go. That left little mental energy to ponder why a body would be out on the point.

The sand was cold. Beaches in Northern California were never terribly warm, but as St. Patrick's Day inched closer, the chill of winter lingered despite the hint of spring in the air.

As Thor sensed some heat left in the corpse, Doris tried in vain to prevent him from jumping atop the cadaver.

"Stupid cat." Doris sat there while Thor warmed his furry rear end.

Two local students from Clouston College walked by.

"Look at the size of that cat!" The tall woman let go of her companion's hand, and raised her cell phone. "I have to capture this. It'll make a great post."

"Is that a body?" her friend asked, her voice trembling.

They moved closer. The one with the cell phone talked as she walked around the corpse and the cat. "While walking on the beach this morning, we came across this dead body."

"How do we know it's dead?" Her friend leaned in for a closer look. "Is it a prank? A dummy?"

"Poke it, Lissa."

Lissa did. "Yup. Dead. Eeew! Why aren't you upset?" She turned as if to run.

"Medical student." The one with the cell grabbed her hand, pulled her back. "Stay put." She resumed her video. "First one I've seen in the wild. Y'know, outside of a morgue or lab for class. Really interesting. Look at the eyes…" She leaned closer, holding her phone close to the dead woman's face.

"Not sure I want to hold your hand again!" Lissa said.

"Sure you do." The medical student winked over her cell phone. "You do know I dissect these for class, right? You wouldn't want to have a surgeon work on you if they hadn't practiced."

Discussion of cutting open bodies was enough for Doris, particularly since she had long been divested of her own body by death. Finally able to take control, Doris steered Thor in the general direction of home.

She even managed to get him to trot a bit.

Chapter 1

George Ho, my favorite cop and old college boyfriend, slammed the front section of the local newspaper down on my trestle table and rapped his knuckle on the picture of a large black cat sitting on a body. "Yours, I presume, Cass?"

I pulled back at the tension in his voice and tried to deflect. "Hard to tell from that grainy picture. I'm tempted to say, 'The body or the cat?'"

He wasn't having any. "Really think there are a lot of thirty pound black cats with amber eyes around this town?"

"Hard to tell his weight from—"

"Just stop."

The dismissal in his tone hurt.

I looked up at my ceiling. "Doris!"

"You rang?" Her head appeared next to the ceiling fan as if she were trying to stay out of reach.

"Why were you perched on a dead body? Why did you make my cat sit on a dead body?"

"I didn't. He didn't want to expose his bottom to the cold sand. You know how he is."

I closed my eyes. I never could get a straight answer out of my resident ghost. She delighted in subterfuge.

George raised an arched, black eyebrow at Doris. "You didn't think about coming back and telling Cass to report it? We had to learn about it from a social media post." He turned to me. "If you have any doubt that it was your cat, I suggest you watch this." He pulled out his phone and played a video that a student had posted.

I opened one eye and winced at the image. "Yeah, that's my baby boy."

George snorted. "What is it with you and bodies on the beach?"

"Hey! Not my beach! That's over on campus." Then I saw a hint of the smile he was trying to suppress. "Oh, yeah. Give me a hard time. See if I ever invite you over for dinner again." I cleared my throat and asked the question I feared. "I can't tell from the photo or video. Was it anyone I know?"

He grimaced. "Possibly. She's…was a small business owner, and you've been creating websites for local businesses. Genevieve Olieson, Genevieve Genealogy?"

I closed my eyes again, a lump forming in my throat, and sat down hard. "I know her. I really like… liked her. I have a contract with her." My mind ricocheted from thought to thought. "Does her niece know?"

"I wouldn't be here if we hadn't contacted next of kin."

"Is she all right? I don't really know her. I've dealt with Gen."

George raised that lovely eyebrow again. His gorgeousness hadn't diminished in the years since we'd been in college together. I must have been an idiot to break up with him back then. His hair was shorter, but still as black as Thor's fur.

"Stupid question. Of course, she isn't. I should call her. Is it too soon?"

George put his phone down and hugged me. "Take a breath. Even though you don't know her well, you can call and offer condolences. Having a contract with her aunt is a perfect reason for a call."

"I don't know if Tina will want to continue or not, but you're right. I can use that as an excuse to tell her how much I liked her aunt and will miss working with her. Oh, I'll have to tell Ricardo and Mia. At least they've already made their tuition payments, but I know they were counting on this contract." A thousand thoughts played tag in my brain.

"Don't go the doom and gloom route yet." George glanced up.

Doris had started to fade like the Cheshire Cat.

"Stop right there," he said as if he had the power to stop a ghost from vanishing.

His attempt to control the situation almost made me forget the body. Last year, this man, who now was trying to order a ghost around, had been so superstitious that the very thought of being in the same room with a spirit would have turned his golden-brown Hawaiian tan pale with fear. Even though he wasn't looking at me, I smiled at him.

Doris solidified, shrank, and sat on the ceiling fan blade, swinging her legs back and forth like a little kid in miniature.

"I need details. What did you notice?" He glowered at her.

"Seriously? You're going to write up an interview with a ghost and put it in an official police record?" she asked.

5

"No, I'm going to write up a report on hearsay from a reluctant, unnamed witness. Now. Details."

Doris drifted downward, enlarging as she landed. "Body was still warm. That's why Thor hopped aboard. When he looked at her, I could see her clearly. Being a cat, he's nearsighted, of course, so although we heard footsteps, the world beyond the beach was blurry. Not sure about colors, but you have the body. What was left of the dress was in shreds around her. It looked blue, but everything looks blue by moonlight. Plus, cats have limited color vision, which I'm sure you already know."

George looked at me.

I shrugged. Actually, I'd had no idea.

"Her hair was burnished. Um. I'd describe it as antique gold. Rich. Loved the thick braid with the ribbon woven in. Oh, and unique—to me anyway—piercings." She thought for a moment. "Dark spots. Could have been tattoos of birds. Small. Delicate. Given Thor's eyesight, I can't be more specific."

"Bats."

"What?" I'd met her, and I didn't recall any tattoos. Bats seemed like an out-of-character choice for her. She'd been so professional when we went over the contract.

George looked up from the notes he was writing instead of recording her. Doris' relationship to electronic devices was iffy.

"They were bats, and you wouldn't have seen them if her dress had been in one piece. They were small and in interesting places. Please don't repeat this, and, no, I won't tell you where they are because it's info we may use."

"She lay on her back. We didn't see wounds or

blood." Doris frowned. "She smelled funny. Unpleasant."

George looked up. "Cats make very bad witnesses."

"Do you want to hear this or not?" Doris crossed her arms and manifested a pair of glasses with tortoise shell frames perched on her nose. "Thor needs glasses. Are all cats red-green colorblind?"

"No idea. You heard footsteps. Heavy? Light? Scuffling? Heels?"

"Thor has excellent hearing. I'd say furtive." Doris ran her slender, pale fingers through her dark bob.

"Interesting. There aren't any security cameras on the shore side of the observatory. There's a drop-off to the beach and no entrance or walkway on that side."

I got up, poured coffee, and set a mug in front of George. "Have you talked to Frank Wright, Gen's assistant? I know you talked to her niece." I stirred sugar and cream into my cup.

"Thanks." He sipped gingerly. "We haven't been able to reach him. We've been told he's out of town visiting his mother."

"Did you try his cell?" I sat with my own mug of coffee and tucked my chestnut brown hair behind my ears.

George nodded. "It appears to be turned off. My guess would be he's in a movie theater or restaurant. Something like that."

"I never turn mine off."

He smirked. "Yes, I know."

"You can silence them."

"Some people take breaks from their electronics."

I quit. It wasn't worth an argument that couldn't be

resolved.

George leaned back and slapped his hands on his knees. "You and bodies."

"It wasn't me! I didn't find it." I waved in Doris' direction. "They did."

Then I saw the upward curve of lips. Still teasing. That was a good sign. Our relationship had been a bit touch and go lately. To me, he seemed distant and abrupt, but every now and then he'd surprise me with a smile or a compliment. It put me on edge, making me uncertain. Was he still upset about our past or was something else was going on?

He folded up his notebook and tucked it back into his pocket. "Would it do any good to tell you to stay away and not to poke around?" He stood.

I got up, too. "George, sweetie, she was my customer. I do need to talk to Frank and Tina at the very least to find out if CaRiMia still has a job with them." I paused. "And I liked her, so I want to know what happened to her."

One side of his mouth tightened and his eyes narrowed, signs I now associated with an internal debate. "You will tell me whatever you find out. You will be discreet. You will not interfere with the investigation."

"Yes, sir." I almost saluted.

"Huh. See you later."

I caught the shadow of a smile as he left.

I closed the door behind him and faced Doris. "You'd think that ghosts would haunt their murderers. Word would get around, and the murder rate would drop."

"It doesn't work like that."

"You mean because ghosts are tied to a place? The murderer could pack up and move."

She shrugged. "As far as I know, there's no handbook. You could be tied to an object, I suppose, but a lot of us don't remember who killed us."

"That's inconvenient." Then another thought occurred to me. "Did you happen to see her ghost?"

"Did I just mention there isn't a handbook? I didn't see her, and I don't know when someone's spirit hangs around and when it goes into the light." She sighed. "If I did…"

An oddly hollow sensation at the thought of her leaving nearly overwhelmed me. I'd be lonely. Living with a ghost was like having a roommate for company but without the dirty dishes or laundry. "It was a thought. You found that other ghost on the beach."

"She had unfinished business. When she finished it—*pfft*—she was gone."

Doris' ability to morph her appearance to match her emotional state amazed me. In a flash, she went from red lips, long eyelashes around blue eyes, and curly dark hair to sallow skin, pale lips, straight hair, and nearly gray eyes. The picture of someone in mourning.

"Wouldn't Gen have unfinished business if she'd been murdered?" I asked.

"We don't know how she died."

"George is investigating, so it's bound to be a suspicious death. She was lying there dead and all in the middle of the night. Long after the observatory closed, which would have been the only place she could have fallen from. Can't think of an accident that would shred her dress. Yes, I will ask George if she was sexually assaulted although he wasn't in the mood to discuss details with me. But if it were something like that, he'd have warned me to be careful instead of telling me not to poke my nose in."

"True. Or he's calling it a murder as an excuse to see you." She transformed into a flirty flapper.

I smiled in spite of myself. "He doesn't need an excuse."

Doris waved at me as she faded out with a shimmy and a shake.

Back to finding out where we stood on the contract for Gen's business. I took my cell off the charger in the kitchen, topped off my mug, and sat to make some calls. I hesitated because Gen's niece was top of the list. I couldn't swallow for a moment, but I had to do this.

She answered immediately. "Genevieve Genealogy. Tina Dewey speaking."

"Hi, Tina. This is Cass Peake. We met last week at Gen's office."

"You're the website designer. I'll add you to contacts."

"That's right."

Tina hesitated. "Do you know…?"

"Yes, that's why I'm calling. I wanted to offer you my condolences. I hadn't known your aunt long, but I liked her and was looking forward to doing business with her." I doodled a heart on my notepad.

She hesitated and then said, "Thank you."

I hurried on. "Gen mentioned that you're her niece and that she was preparing you to be her partner. I wondered if you were planning to run the business and if you still have need of the website and services she contracted for?"

"I'm sure you understand that I don't want to presume that the business is mine. I know she had a will with a lawyer in town, but I'll have to wait to see what's in it before I can make any decisions. Can we put a hold on things until I know more?"

"Yes, of course. I'm so sorry for your loss. I really enjoyed talking to your aunt. I would have liked to work with her." I winced when I realized I'd repeated myself. I wanted to sound competent, not inane. Ricardo, Mia, and I had barely gotten our company off the ground. I wanted it to fly high.

"Thank you so much. I really miss her. I'll call you when I know more, Ms. Peake."

"Call me Cass. Talk to you then." I ended the call.

Time to call Ricardo and Mia and break the bad news.

When I reached him, Ricardo sounded tired. "The timing is lousy," he said after I told him about Gen's death.

"I'm sure Gen thought so, too." Ricardo was usually more sensitive than this. Had something happened? "Why? What's up?"

I heard his intake of breath. Something was definitely wrong.

"I'll tell you later. In person." Again, he hesitated. "About the murder…"

Murder. Ricardo assumed it was murder just as I had, but George hadn't actually used the word. What else could it be? Her clothing was ripped. I didn't want to think about what that might mean.

"Cass? You there?"

"Sorry. Yes, I'm here. George left a bit ago. He didn't say that it was murder, but he was pretty mad

11

that a video of Thoris sitting on the body had been posted online."

"Thoris? What does Doris know about the murder? I'll have to look for that video. Do you have a link?"

"Sorry. No link. George showed me. Doris doesn't know much. She pointed out that my cat is nearsighted and colorblind-ish. She's a lousy witness. But yes, it sounds like murder. I liked her. Gen." My chest felt tight.

"I was looking forward to working on this one. I love creaky old Victorian mansions." He sounded tired.

"Don't give up hope yet, Ricardo. I still think you should take the photos. If Tina inherits, we'll have to move quickly to get a memorial for Gen up. In the meantime, I thought I'd beat the bushes for more business."

Ricardo gave a small chuckle. "While you're abusing the flora, you might go up the coast a bit to some of the other towns."

"Good idea. Gotta go. I want to invite Jack and Gillian for St Patrick's. You guys should come by while they're here."

"Thanks. We will. Talk to you later."

My final call was to my brother Jack, who told me to quit finding bodies. This time I pled innocent and told him it was all his fault because the cat he gave me when his landlord found out about Thor and threatened to evict him was the culprit who found the body.

"We're coming over for St. Patrick's Day. We're taking most of the week and staying with you as usual."

My younger brother always assumed he was welcome, and he was right. "Looking forward to it. I'll even fold all the laundry that's littering the bed."

Jack snorted. "And lay in a supply of that amazing hard cider while you're at it."

"Will do. Let me know when you leave and drive carefully." I hung up and noticed Doris watching me, her chin resting on her upturned palms, elbows on the table. "Isn't it boring hanging around, watching the living?"

Back to her perky self, Doris raised an arched, perfectly penciled à la the Twenties eyebrow. "What makes you think we hang around?"

"I know you take my cat for…" The image of Thor sitting on the corpse flitted through my only-moderately-caffeinated brain.

She nodded. "Uh-huh. I can see the thought forming. Yes, I was looking for a bit more excitement than you provide. Who wants to sit around watching the living paint their nails when I can…" She swished a hand through the air and then fanned her fingers across her face, displaying five perfectly manicured, magenta nails with tiny, pink hearts on each.

I ground my teeth and glanced at my own sloppy polish job. "I have to go out and scavenge for some more website and promo work if I want to keep eating and paying for electricity and manicures. I can't ask Mia and Ricardo to take time off from classes and studying to do it. Ricardo's right. It's time to do a little coastal exploring. See what's going on in the other small towns along Highway 1." I tucked my cell phone into my crossbody bag. "So, you won't have to be bored by me today."

"Y'know, the California coast has quite a history. In this area, there was a lot of bootlegging." Her outfit changed to a red cloche hat and a long, straight, cloth coat with a big fur collar.

"That's right! Wasn't your father a bootlegger before you all were—" I drew a finger across my throat. "What can you tell me?"

She winced and put a hand to her throat at my gesture. "When you go pick up the hard cider, ask them about their ghosts."

Chapter 2

The distillery that produced the hard cider that Jack had requested squatted on a rocky outcropping two towns north of Las Lunas. I set out to pick some up but also to scout out new business and the ghosts that Doris had mentioned. Maybe the distillery would like a bit of help gaining a wider audience for their delicious products.

The nippy air cleared my head, and I relaxed as I drove through the small towns that blended together along the ocean, punctuated here and there by the remaining farms. Cerulean blue waves glimmered in the sunlight. I smiled. I'd be back for the peas. Peas grown here were the sweetest I'd ever eaten. Peas like it cool, so the spring climate on the coast is perfect. Sad to think that these farms would soon be lost to monster, view-blocking mansions.

I slowed as I passed Gen's. My ebullient mood faded a bit. Although Tina had owned the business with her aunt, Gen was the one with the reputation for spot-on ancestor searches. She had all the right instincts for digging out clues in someone's history to uncover their story in the past. Tina's expertise ran more to the business end of things. Gen's larger-than-life personality had dwarfed Tina's careful precision. I wondered if the caterpillar would turn into a butterfly now that she was in control.

I tried to put my worries aside as tires crunched the gravel in the parking lot at the distillery. The area near the entrance was empty. That was to be expected this early in the day. Employee parking must be further away. I left my car near the front door and went in.

This place was no one's idea of a haunted house. The interior spaces were cool, industrial, and open with a squeaky-clean feel as if someone had taken a squeegee to them. I sniffed and caught a vaguely alcoholic citrus smell, but that could have been cleaning fluid.

Before I'd moved to the coast from Pleasanton on the other side of San Francisco Bay after my divorce from the evil Phil, I would have said that an establishment such as this, with no gothic, spooky atmosphere, couldn't possibly house a ghost. Living with Doris had totally changed my attitude, so I looked into the dark corners and even up at the beams to see if I was being watched. I smiled. I probably was but by security guards, not ghosts. Nothing but security cameras in the rafters.

I jumped and turned swiftly when someone said hello behind me.

"Oh, sorry. Didn't mean to startle you." A small, slender woman with long, straight black hair wiped her hands on a bar towel and smiled up at me.

"I heard you had a ghost…"

Her eyes narrowed, but the smile remained. "And you thought a ghost would be up there?" She pointed skyward.

I suddenly realized that it might have looked as though I were casing the joint. I hesitated. I couldn't very well say, "Well, my ghost likes to sit on my ceiling fan blades." So, I said, "I was admiring the wide-open spaces."

Her head tilted and her mouth skewed to one side. Plainly, she didn't believe me.

I cleared my throat and pulled a card out of my pocket. "I know you're not open until noon. I'll be back to make a purchase later. My brother is visiting and loves your hard cider." I tried for a confidential tone. "However, my partners and I have a business down in Las Lunas." I handed our CaRiMia business card to her. "We design websites among other things."

She raised an eyebrow.

I hurried on. "I've seen your website with the history of the place as a speakeasy. Bootleggers." I could use a drink about now. I'd have to do better with the promotion of our little company, but recently, our customers had been small, single-owner shops. The distillery was well established and known outside our local area. This was the sort of business we needed to bring in if we were going to expand our company sufficiently to provide a decent living for the three of us. My dreams even extended to hiring an assistant.

She smiled. "We're quite well known. You might say a tourist attraction."

I pointed at the card she held. "There's a list of some of our clients on the other side." Truth was it was the entire list of our clients so far. "Have a look when you get the chance. I'll be back." Did I hear a faint chuckle above me as I left?

I stopped next at the candle shop a couple miles up the highway. I didn't cold call on the phone because it was just that...cold. Uncomfortable as the last visit had been for me, I preferred the personal touch. Dropping by allowed me to gain an impression of the business. My feelings about a store started at the curb. This owner had taken the time to create an inviting store front. The two shop windows were well-dressed in a rainbow of color. Candles of all sizes and shapes and colors sat on perches of stone, wood, or draped fabric in neutral shades.

I entered the shop and breathed in deeply. Lilac. Vanilla. Sandalwood. I'm so glad I don't have a fragrance allergy like my cousin in New York. Although the scent of flowers doesn't bother her, something in the artificial odors sends her into spasms. I love scented candles, so walking into this shop was heaven. I embraced the rainbow of colors and garden of scents. It was a bit of a touch desert, though. I'd have to go to a yarn shop for my tactile fix. Good thing there was one on today's list.

As I left the shop a half hour later, I ticked them off my list. Their business was largely walk-in, and their margin too slim for a promotional budget beyond word of mouth, social media, and flyers at this point. I got that.

Same story at the yarn shop, although they'd started classes and a Knit for your Kneighbors group to make clothing and afghans for people in need, and might want a simple website for schedules and contacts. Social media worked better for them than a website because of flexibility. Although their clientele spanned the generations, their regular customers tended to be older. Not all were media savvy. I'd have to think about possible solutions to increase the store's reach to other potential customers. While I was there and talking to the owner, I strolled around the shop, stroking as many skeins as I could, lingering over the seafoam green alpaca a bit longer than necessary. Back in the car, I doodled knitting needles with a question mark next to their name.

I finished my rounds and headed back toward the distillery around noon to buy the cider for Jack.

The woman I'd talked to earlier greeted me with a smile this time. She now wore a name tag that read Emica.

"Call me Emmy. Everyone does." She led me toward the back bar area. "After you left, we had a little meeting about an upcoming event, and there is something you can do for us. We've been part of this community for nearly a century in one form or another. There's going to be a coastal ghost hop." We stopped at the counter, and she signaled a man. "We want to be part of it but also promote our uniqueness and longevity in the area."

He brought over a sheaf of papers.

She took the papers from him. "What was it you wanted to purchase?"

"Your hard cider."

She nodded to the man, who walked off. "Now, we'd like to talk about publicity to go with the ghost hop but also a campaign leading up to the date on which we opened a century ago. Would you be interested?"

"We would." Bonanza! I tried not to shriek.

"Here are some ideas to work with. Background. Copies of photos. Stuff that isn't on the current website. Also," she pulled a paper out of the sheaf, "we'll have a presence on the ghost hop site. They've asked us to design our own page. Each stop has a page. We'd like you to do that." Placing the ghost hop info on top, she handed the papers to me. "This," she tapped the top sheet, "is their information. That will give you an idea of the flavor of the event."

I saw the twinkle in her eye as she said, conspiratorially leaning forward, "If you're interested in ghosts, you might also like to participate."

"Definitely." I returned her smile. "This is excellent. I'll present to my partners and be back with a contract."

The man returned, setting two cardboard carryalls of cider on the counter.

"With our compliments. We want you to sample our product to better promote our interests." She tapped the top of a can. "This is our most popular, and this," she flicked a finger at the other carryall, "is something new we're trying. Please let us know what you think."

"I will, with pleasure." I tucked the paperwork under my arm and picked up the cider. "Thank you. Thank you very much."

She ushered me to my car. "We look forward to working with you." She waved as I drove off.

When I got home, I pulled up onto a sandy patch in front of my little blue and burgundy Craftsman bungalow and got out.

"Mina! Nice to see you." I grabbed the cider and headed toward my porch where my elderly neighbor sat on the porch swing, wrapped in a pale lilac ruana.

"I have a small mystery I'd like you to solve. Very small." She cocked her head to one side like a quizzical great blue heron.

"You know I'm happy to help in any way I can. C'mon in. It's chilly out here." I set the cider down, opened the door, and held it for her, picking up the cider and following her in.

She settled herself at my old trestle table in the kitchen while I stashed the bottles in the fridge in anticipation of Jack and Gillian's arrival.

"Do you know the difference between a ghost and a spirit?"

"Tea?" I asked.

"Please."

I dropped the paperwork on the table and filled the kettle, knowing Mina preferred brewed tea. "Aren't they the same thing?"

Mina shook her head. "No, my dear, not quite. You see, a ghost is stuck here, but a spirit has merely come to visit for a while." Her gray eyes were the color of the mid-March fog wisping about on the beach in the evening. "Often with a warning or a message."

I frowned. "I know you're sensitive. Can't you ask it what it wants?"

A small smile curled the outer edges of her mouth. "Not really. All Prissy does is meow."

I nearly choked. "A cat ghost?"

"Yes, of course. Did you think humans were a special case?"

"I don't know what I thought." I measured the loose tea to give myself time to think, but my memories of discussions of ghosts didn't provide any clues. I didn't think Doris had ever mentioned animal ghosts.

"Humans can be self-centered, don't you agree? I rather think that life is life. We need to accept it in all its varied and interesting forms."

I put a plate of shortbread in front of her. "Even if that life is a dead cat ghost?"

21

"Just so."

I set her favorite flowered porcelain cup in its saucer on the table. The cup had been in the back of a cupboard when I first bought the house. Mina exclaimed over its beauty on one of her visits. I offered it to her, but she said she'd get much more pleasure by visiting it on occasion.

"Even more interesting in old age." Mina ran her finger around the rim of the cup. "But Prissy is not the sort of creature you'd expect to be haunted by." Mina met my gaze. "Which is why I believe she's a spirit, not a ghost, and why we must find out why she's paid me a visit."

"And we can't ask her."

Mina shook her head. "No, Cass, we cannot." She sipped her tea.

I nodded. "I think this might be a case for Thoris to solve."

"Of course." Her laugh lines became more pronounced. "A human ghost possessing a cat to communicate with a spirit cat. If that doesn't work, I don't know what will."

I remembered Mina's nervous first visit inside my house after I'd moved in. She'd seemed terrified of Doris back then. But here she was, asking for Doris' help. "Did you just manipulate me?"

She cocked her head. "I brought you your favorite lemon bars. Is that what you call manipulation?" She reached into a capacious canvas bag to retrieve a tin covered in a rose pattern that she handed to me.

I took it from her and had to admit that I liked her methods. "Feel free to make me bow to your will with lemon bars as much as you like."

She laughed. "I look forward to Thoris' visit." She set her empty cup down and rose.

I walked her out and watched her glide up the hill toward her tall Victorian. Then I turned to look out at the choppy Pacific Ocean. How do I communicate with a ghost cat? I corrected myself, a spirit cat. I strolled slowly down toward the water's edge. I'd thrown every cent from my divorce settlement with Phil at my little bungalow. So far, CaRiMia, the website business I'd started with Mia and Ricardo plus the little windfall from some gemstones that I'd found hidden in my loft had kept me afloat financially, but after Christmas, business had fallen off rather drastically. The peeling burgundy, navy, and white trim was a silent reproach for my neglect. I needed to raise the money for upkeep. I averted my gaze and climbed the steps back to my porch. One last, deep breath of salty sea air and I entered.

Two problems. How to earn some money for the empty coffers and how to communicate with a spirit cat. If Mina was right and Prissy was here to give her a message, the cat would be motivated to give us answers. Is a spirit cat smarter than a live cat? Does a cat gain knowledge when it dies? Then I thought of Doris, my resident human ghost and thought better of it. And how does she know its name is Prissy?

"Doris! Want another adventure?" I called into the ether.

She appeared dressed as Sherlock Holmes.

"Seriously?"

She shook herself, and her clothes morphed into classic Thirties' Nancy Drew.

"Better. I take it you overheard my conversation

with Mina."

She nodded. "I'm ready to go, but I need to possess your live cat and become Thoris so that I can talk to a dead cat." She dramatically raised the back of her hand to her forehead as she faded out, saying, "I'm so confused…"

"Drama queen," I muttered and sat down at my computer to start on the contract for the distillery.

****

I'd finished the contract and was grilling a cheese sandwich when Thoris returned a few hours later.

Doris made a great show of wiggling her way out of Thor's body as if it were a girdle or a tight pair of pants and enlarging to my size.

Thor stalked off in search of food.

Doris shimmied in a silver fringed dress, looking like a dog shaking off water. "I may move in with Mina."

"Oh? What does she have that I don't?" I flipped my sandwich over.

"She fed us shrimp and cream." Doris hugged herself. "She set out a velvet cushion for us to sit on. She stroked us and told us we were beautiful."

"Cream! Oh, no! Milk, cream, ice cream—they're all terrible for cats. I'll be cleaning up messes for days." I'd almost forgotten their purpose in going. "So, what did you find out? Did you meet Prissy?" I slipped the sandwich onto a waiting plate.

"That's not her name. It's—" She trilled.

"Pretty name. Not sure I can pronounce it. Did she tell you what she wants?" I pulled out a steak knife and sawed the sandwich in half, the gooey Swiss cheese slipping out onto the plate.

24

Doris batted her eyelashes. "I'll have to go back to find out."

"You just want more shrimp." I grabbed a napkin and a cold glass of milk and sat at the trestle table.

"Beats canned cat food." She vanished in a puff of glitter—fortunately, ghost glitter.

"Great. At least I won't have to vacuum." I bit into the warm deliciousness.

Chapter 3

I knew from experience that I wouldn't get anything out of Doris until she was ready to divulge it. If Doris was ungrateful, perhaps my partners would value the work I'd done on their behalf today. I finished my sandwich and glanced at my watch. Mia was still in her lab, but Ricardo should be at the Crystal Shop. I called his cell instead of the shop number.

"Hey! We had some good luck today. I'd like to work on it a bit this afternoon and then present it to you and Mia. Want to come over for dinner and bring Mia? I could run it all by you then."

"Free meal? Sure! Okay if I bring another person?"

"Do I know this person?"

"Not yet. She's my folklore professor. Visiting professor. Started this semester. Doesn't know anyone. Not from here. I thought it would be nice for her."

"Of course. Bring her along. The more the merrier. I know you have classes and work tomorrow, so if you come around five, we can eat, socialize, and do business, and you can be home at a reasonable hour." I rang off, put my plate and glass in the sink, and laid my cell on the kitchen counter.

I opened the fridge and stuck my head inside. I hadn't done any shopping for Jack and Gillian's visit other than the cider, and little was left in my larder. Hmm. For a working dinner, this could be informal. I could do pesto and pasta with sautéed veggies. I did have some parmesan cheese as a little protein topper. I could try out my new micro-shredder. I rummaged for a few minutes and came up with a slightly wilted broccoli crown, an onion, some carrots, a jar of baby corn, sun-dried tomatoes, and a can of great northern beans. That would do. I always kept pasta in various sizes and shapes, but did I have pesto? Aha! Yes, I had sufficient fresh basil pesto. I personally loved sun-dried tomato pesto, which is probably why I was out of it.

Feeling more secure about dinner, I settled down to work on the material from the distillery.

At a quarter to five, I started chopping veggies for a tossed salad while the pasta cooked.

As the doorbell rang, I dumped the fusilli in the strainer to drain. After drying my hands on my new shamrock towel I'd impulsively purchased last week for the holiday, I went to open the door.

Mia, Ricardo, and a tall, young woman with an amazing shock of dark brown, curly hair and hazel eyes stood on my stoop. She belied the stereotype of a professor that had popped into my head when Ricardo mentioned her profession. Mia and Ricardo reminded me of the little Scottie dog magnets—one black and one white—with opposite magnetic pull. Mia's short stature contrasted with Ricardo's tall muscularity. His long, black hair pulled severely back in a ponytail at the nap of his neck while Mia's short, platinum hair curled around her face.

I held the door wide. "C'mon in. Your timing is perfection. Dinner's ready." I hurried to the kitchen, saying over my shoulder, "Good thing, too, because I have no appetizers. Don't mean to be rude. Mia and

Ricardo know their way around."

I put the noodles into the waiting serving dish and carried them out to the dining table to set them on a trivet. "Ricardo, can you manage drinks while I get the rest of the food?"

"Sure thing." He followed me into the kitchen. "What do you have?"

"I made some spiced iced tea. The pitcher's in the fridge. There's also some cider, beer, and a bottle of red."

"Gotcha."

I made quick work of reducing the wedge of parmesan to a pile of such tiny cheese threads that it resembled ivory cotton candy.

We both made a couple of trips to and fro before settling down at the table.

I looked up and realized how rude I'd been. "Oh, my gosh! I'm so so sorry! It's been a day and a half. Seriously, I feel like I've crammed thirty-six hours into twenty-four. I'm Cass Peake. Welcome to my home, such as it is."

The woman's laughter pealed like a sonorous bell. She was an alto with a low, rich voice. "Don't worry. I'm Dani Boyd, visiting prof up at the college. I feel right at home. I get distracted easily myself. You should see my office. Total chaos." She nodded toward Ricardo. "He can tell you. We'll be in the middle of a conversation, and I'll wander off to look something up and totally forget he's in my office."

I looked over at Ricardo. He raised his eyebrows and nodded.

"I'm delighted you let me come to dinner. I like meeting people who are outside the academic arena."

Dani smiled, displaying a dimple in her right cheek. "I have many interests, not all academic. For example, I'm a forager. Are you familiar with the movement?"

Mia lit the candles and got the pepper grinder I'd forgotten.

"I know what foraging is. Admittedly, most of mine takes place at the market."

Dani leaned forward on her elbows. "I grew up on a farm in a part of Indiana so rural that the nearest post office was Hicksville, Ohio."

I couldn't help it. I laughed.

She mock-frowned at me. "Don't laugh. I know how it sounds, but Major Hicks was a Revolutionary War hero."

That made me laugh even harder. I noticed that Mia and Ricardo smiled but managed not to guffaw.

She ignored my mirth. "It was a great place to grow up. I had my own horse. My parents were into Euell Gibbons and *Stalking the Wild Asparagus*. I spent many summers as a kid, nursing a bad case of poison oak until I got better at identifying plants."

I raised a finger to call a pause. "So, foraging is getting rashes in Indiana?"

Again, Dani's laughter pealed over us. "Thanks. You've made my point and followed me down one of my rabbit trails. I'll take you on a forage. It's easier if I show you what I mean. Trust me. You'll love it, and you'll see parts of California you didn't even know existed."

"We don't have to forage for this meal, so let's eat!" Ricardo passed the pasta.

Mia helped herself to the roasted veggies and handed them to Dani.

"I hope we're not putting you out." Dani nodded toward Ricardo. "Ricardo's in one of my classes. He's kindly been filling me in on some of the local legends. He mentioned something about ghosts, and I was hooked. I'm so glad you were open to having me join you all this evening."

"If you're interested in ghosts, then you shouldn't be too bored by my presentation to Mia and Ricardo. It's not as formal as it sounds, but language is important, and I want us to be in the habit of using appropriate terminology instead of lapsing into verbiage so that we do it automatically when we have more clients than we can handle and have hit the big time."

She nodded. "Agreed. It's also good for these guys to get used to doing presentations."

Ricardo groaned.

"You especially," Dani said. "You'll have to sell yourself to make a living. Mia will have an easier time. Her tech skills are awesome."

Mia smiled.

Dani looked around. "This is a lovely little Craftsman house. Have you lived here long?"

I shook my head as I added some fluffy parmesan to my helping. "No, as a matter of fact. I'm nearly as new as you are to the area. I moved over from Pleasanton after my divorce from my ex last summer, I met Ricardo and Mia on the beach here." I flashed back to the "vampire" killing for a moment. "That was quite an autumn."

Ricardo helped himself to the cheese and passed the bowl to Mia. "We all became friends and formed the company I was telling you about. Mia's our tech wiz."

Mia passed the bread to Dani. "As our most mature partner, Cass does our presentations except when one of us has a better in with a potential client."

Dani ground fresh pepper on her salad. "So, three of you can make a living from doing website design?"

I cringed at the minginess of the salad and took only a small portion for myself. "So far. Things are a bit tight right about now, so I was out flogging the shrubbery for business again today. We picked up a small contract."

Dani took a sip of her iced tea. "Tuition isn't cheap." She looked at Ricardo and Mia. "Two students."

"There is that. Ricardo's been known to work multiple jobs." I noticed Ricardo and Mia exchanging a look.

"Better tell her," Mia said. "She's frowning at us."

I hadn't realized I'd frowned. "Tell me what?"

"Ricardo isn't working as many jobs." She elbowed him.

He shrugged. "Samantha fired me."

I dropped my fork. "No! I don't believe it. She counts on you."

"Go on," Mia prompted him.

"Uhh. Apparently, I'm male."

"No kidding. She just realized that?" I asked.

"She wants to hire a college female. She said I'm part of the patriarchy."

Mia leaned forward. "She's moved out of Brendan's." She grinned. "I guess she noticed he's male, too."

"That's too bad. I had high hopes for that pairing, and I thought she loved that beautiful old Victorian as much as he does!" I turned to Dani. "I'm sorry. I didn't mean to cut you out of the conversation."

"No, this is fascinating. Go on." She dusted her pasta with parmesan.

"Samantha Ross owns the Crystal Shop in town."

"I've been in there. She has some wonderful earrings."

I nodded. "That's the one. Brendan Mays owns the bookstore Dreams and Dust. He inherited a lovely Victorian house when his father died, and Samantha moved in with him. I think he said it was a Queen Anne. The two are…were great together." My mind revisited the delicious dinners I'd enjoyed with them there. "Samantha often moves rapidly from one interest to another. Mind like quicksilver."

"Look, I know I don't know either party, but from what I'm hearing, I'm not sure this has anything to do with you, Ricardo. I think she might be indulging in some all-or-nothing thinking after breaking up with Brendan. I don't think she's really rejecting you. I think she's off men…temporarily."

I looked at Dani with new eyes. "That's how I felt when Phil cheated on me. That all men are rats."

Dani nodded. "I think Brendan did something or didn't do something that upset her emotionally." Dani pulled a small, black notebook from her bag and scribbled a few notes. "Normally, I'd use the notes app and voice function on my cell. But that would be rude at dinner. Let's see. Samantha Ross. The Crystal Shop on Main. Dreams and Dust." She tucked her notebook away. "I'm still getting the lay of the land here. Two shops to visit with new eyes, and two people to get to know."

I wondered, but I let it drop. "If you like, we could meet for lunch at the new crêpe place and do a bit of shopping. I'm happy to introduce you to Samantha and Brendan. Might break some ice."

"I'd love that. Thank you."

I turned to Ricardo and Mia. "I had a thought. Ricardo, why don't you give her a bit of space to miss you and remember what you did for her. Even if she hires someone else, she'll remember that you could practically read her mind and anticipate what she needed done."

Mia put her hand on Ricardo's. "He had to sell his car for tuition. It might mean that she won't let the company do the website as long as he's involved."

"Ask for more money when she rehires you," Dani said.

He looked back and forth between Mia and myself as if Dani weren't there. "She probably won't use CaRiMia if any men are involved. Look, it's probably better if I quit."

I put both my hands on the table. "Nope. You aren't going anywhere, Ricardo. For starters, you're an equal partner. Plus, we've got a smallish job with the distillery to do their publicity for the Ghost Hop. I've actually got a slide show for you all with some mockups. I finished writing up the contract if you like my ideas and want to move ahead. Then you can have a look before I take it over to them." I explained as quickly as I could so as not to bore Dani. "So, you see, we'll be fine. Besides, we won't be blackmailed. Right, Mia?"

Mia nodded. "Right!"

Out of the corner of my eye, I saw Dani stiffen.

Her eyes widened when I mentioned blackmail. I briefly wondered why.

"And tomorrow morning, I'll give Tina a call to see if she's ready to discuss the contract we'd had with Gen." I worried about Ricardo and his having to sell his car for tuition. I didn't want to push someone who was grieving, but I wanted to get the deposit check and give it to him. I thought Mia would be okay with that. Now, if Tina would honor the contract... I didn't even want to consider the possibility that she wouldn't inherit. "As far as Samantha goes, Mia and I will be her contacts for a while."

Dani leaned forward, listening. I realized that she was an observer by nature.

"Samantha is already into Celtic mythology. We created the wheel of Celtic holidays for her website so that she could emphasize different jewelry and crystals at different times of the year. Remember her Yule campaign? Let's mention that we're already planning for next year. Mia, you could suggest a St. Brigid's campaign, emphasis on Brigid—the Divine Feminine. It's a month earlier at the beginning of February, called Imbolc on the wheel if you remember the six equidistant points, so her sales and campaign will precede both Valentine's Day and St. Patrick's. She could increase her sales for both holidays. What do you think? Would it be enough to keep her as a customer?"

Mia pursed her lips. "It might work."

"Let's hope Brendan figures out what he did wrong and makes it up to her." I snuffed out the candles. "Let's move into the living room where we'll be more comfortable, and I'll show you what I've got. Any suggestions are welcome. From you, too, Dani."

Chapter 4

That night I dreamt of Irish gods and goddesses. St. Patrick's Day must have been getting to me. I woke up with a plan. During the night, my brain had incorporated a bunch of disparate threads in my life.

Before she left, Dani pointed out that I could invite both Brendan and Samantha to an Irish party that would honor both St. Brigid and St. Patrick. She said she'd email an article she'd read on how St. Brigid was becoming as popular as St. Patrick in Ireland. My brain wove them together into a tapestry, and I awoke with a plan of sorts. I would bring them together and celebrate both at my party.

It took two cups of coffee and a lot of doodling before the plan took shape. My proposed St. Patrick's Day party would now become an Irish celebration, with a nod to St. Brigid as well. I read the email that Dani sent and then did a few searches on my own to discover that St. Brigid was indeed becoming popular and rivaling St. Patrick at this time of year in Ireland. I couldn't wait to run this idea by Jack and Gillian. We'd have to change up the decorations for my party a bit.

Mia and Ricardo had liked my ideas and added a few of their own. It was too early to take the contract to the distillery, so I spent a few hours researching and planning and didn't realize how much time had passed until the landline rang. I looked at the caller ID.

"Hi, Tina. Good morning."

"Morning, Cass. I'll cut to the chase. I received a preliminary copy of Aunt Gen's autopsy report this morning."

"Do they know the cause of death?"

"She was murdered. Poisoned." Her voice broke on the word. "Left to die alone. In pain."

Tears welled in my eyes as I recalled the video that George had shown me. The reality of it was sinking in, and I could tell from the odd tone in Tina's voice that she was still processing the violence of her aunt's death, too. It would take time for her to work through it. Wait a minute. Poisoned? Left by an observatory? I tried to speak gently. "Did the report say how?"

"Not in a way I could understand, so I talked to one of our contacts. Aunt Gen's known her for a decade, and they've helped each other out. She did some digging and interpreting for me. Aunt Gen was injected with a lethal combination of street drugs."

Injected? Not stabbed or hit over the head? "So, her killer wasn't out to rob her or have his way with her, so to speak, or use her in any other way. He didn't…?"

"No. She wasn't violated if that's what you mean. I have no idea why her clothes were shredded or why she was placed on the other side of the observatory, except maybe to try to hide her for a while. They don't think she was killed there. It's a bit of a mystery." Tina's voice broke.

It was planned. "He or she wanted to eliminate her and did. Drugs and the means to inject them had to be procured. That means the killer had a motive for killing your aunt. The killer could have been a man or a woman but strong enough to move a body."

"But why? I don't understand. Everyone loved Aunt Gen. She reunited families. She made people happy." Tina sobbed. "And she was nice."

"That's why we have to figure out the motive. It's not an obvious one, but where there's a motive there's a way to find out who killed her."

"You can find her killer?" Tina's voice rose at the end of her question and sounded so hopeful that I hated to disappoint her.

I had slipped and used "we." That was a mistake. "That's a job for the police. All I'm saying is that the killer can be discovered and punished. It's possible. A motiveless crime of random violence or quick monetary gain is a lot less likely to be solved when there's no camera or witness."

"Oh." Her voice fell.

"Give them a little time, Tina. I know the detective on the case, and he's very good."

"Thanks." She sighed. "My other piece of news is that the reading of the will is in a few hours. At least I'll know where I stand after that. I thought you'd want to know."

"Thank you. Is there anything I can do for you?"

"Not at the moment, but thanks for asking. I'll let you know when I know anything." She rang off.

I went back to work on my ideas for our Irish get-together, enjoying the myths and thinking up ways to decorate and what color schemes to employ.

****

It was early afternoon before I felt hungry. I'd gotten the guest room straightened and the bathroom cleaned in preparation for Jack and Gillian's visit.

Hunger pangs drove me to the kitchen in search of leftover pasta to heat up. There was just enough for one more meal.

My phone rang. It was Tina again.

"Hi, Tina. Good news?"

"Yes, very good but with some caveats."

"Oh?"

"Final dispensation of property has to wait while the police work to solve Gen's death."

"I hope that doesn't take too long."

"And Frank is furious."

"Why?"

"He says that Aunt Gen promised him that he'd get the business and that I would inherit only the nonbusiness property. The will said that I get everything. There isn't even a suggestion that I should retain Frank as an employee. I think she found out something about him, and he killed her for it. He was in a murderous rage as he left the lawyer's office."

"Don't jump to any conclusions." I wanted to tell her not to say 'murder' so casually.

"She'd changed her will recently, according to Mr. Kane. If what Frank said was true, he might not have known she changed it. I wonder if the lawyer would tell me what the old will said or if that's confidential?"

"It is a hell of a motive." I hesitated. "I hate to ask this, but what does your will say?"

"I don't have one."

"Tina, you live in California. The state will take a huge chunk of your estate if you die intestate. Call the lawyer back and make an appointment to draw up a will."

"You're scaring me. I'll do it now. Bye."

It was as if she'd read my mind. I was thinking that, if what she said was true about Frank's reaction, she would be next if he had a way to secure the company after her death.

But the day wasn't through surprising me.

I opened the note app on my cell phone and tapped the microphone icon. "Today's errands—"

A rambunctious knock at my back door interrupted me.

I looked up to see Frank, with the edge of his hand against the window pane shielding his eyes, peering in at me through the curtains. My heart skipped a beat. I froze for a moment. Shaken, I set my phone down and got up to open the door.

"Hi, Frank. C'mon in." I stepped back to give him room to enter.

He looked around. "Are you alone?"

"Temporarily. My brother will be back soon," I lied for my own protection. "Are you here to discuss the contract?"

His eyes narrowed. "Don't play games with me. I know you talked to Tina." His gaze shifted.

He was lying. I might as well lob the ball into his court.

"Why would I talk to Tina? What happened?"

He straightened and looked straight at me. "I'm here to let you know that we're canceling the contract."

I bit my tongue to keep from telling him that I knew all about the new will. "That's too bad, but I think we'll wait to hear that from Tina."

He ground his teeth. "Listen. You'll deal with me. I'm challenging the will. I had a verbal agreement with Gen. Tina's the one lying to you. She killed Gen before she could change her will in my favor. Tina's the one with the motive to kill her aunt."

What did he think I knew that he'd say things like this? Then I paused. I naturally believed Tina because I liked her better than this aggressive man. But Tina had said that the will had been changed recently. Who was lying?

"If what you say is true, you need to tell the police, not me. I'm surprised you troubled yourself to come here. You could have phoned or, better yet, sent a letter on official company letterhead if you have the power to cancel the contract."

He smiled, but his eyes narrowed. "Now, that wouldn't be very polite. Besides, I want to pick up everything she or Gen gave you. Get it out of your way. It is company property no matter who's running the company."

So that's what he was after. I wondered if Tina had shut him out completely? But I didn't think so. She struck me as essentially timid. This bully wouldn't have any trouble intimidating her. I certainly could see him as a killer. Best to keep what I knew hidden.

I shrugged. "I don't know what you're talking about. I don't have anything that belongs to the company."

He grabbed my upper arm hard enough to leave fingertip-sized bruises. "Don't play games with me. You'll end up regretting it. Remember what happened to Gen."

Was that a confession? My heart beat rapidly as I tried to pull away. "Is that a threat? Are you saying you killed her?"

Chapter 5

He increased the pressure on my arm. "I'm not saying anything to you that you could repeat in court, but you need to forget the contract and back off. The company is mine. Gen promised it to me. Told me the lawyer was drawing up the transfer." He let me go.

He'd said "transfer" not *will*. I knew that she wouldn't transfer her company while she was alive. What was going on? I rubbed my arm.

"Thanks for letting me know your intentions. I'll make sure I'm armed to the teeth the next time I see you wherever I am."

He looked around. "Was that a threat? Did you just threaten me?"

"It's time for you to leave." My hand shook when I opened the back door.

He left without a backward glance.

I locked the door and hurried to the front to make sure that door was locked as well. I rarely locked them during the day.

After my heart quit racing, I went into the bathroom, took my shirt off, and examined the red welts on my upper arm that were already darkening.

I put my shirt back on and tried to think of anything Tina or Gen might have given me that would spur Frank to that kind of violence, but I only had a sheaf of papers about the company's purpose, founding, and other data for the contract we were discussing. What did he think I had?

My cell phone rang. What now?

"Hi, George." I tried to conceal my surprise at his call.

"We've had a complaint."

"Noise? Neighbors?"

He coughed. "It seems you threatened to kill Frank Wright."

Did he call the cops seconds after leaving my house? "Other way around, and I have the bruises to prove it."

"I'll be there in ten minutes."

He arrived fifteen minutes later with Officer Rusty Riordan. Neither smiled as I let them in.

"Coffee?"

"No, thanks," George said. "You mentioned bruises? Officer Riordan will examine you." He was all business.

I led her back to the guest room and took off my shirt to show her my upper arm.

Rusty flipped her auburn braid over her shoulder as she bent to examine my bruises. "I'd like to take photos."

"Go right ahead."

She took out her phone to take pictures and notes. "Have you seen a doctor?"

"Haven't had time. It happened minutes before Geo—Detective Ho called." I related the entire incident.

We walked back to the living room. George looked at the pictures and then read out the complaint.

As he handed Rusty's phone back to her, I had a

sudden flash of memory. "Wait! I might have something…" I picked my phone up from the table. "Yes! I was recording when he barged in."

I tapped on my note and upped the volume. In seconds, Frank's voice rang out in the quiet room.

At the end of the message, George said, "We're gonna need your phone."

"Rats."

He chuckled. "Do you want to counter his claim?"

"Yes." I dumped my phone in the bag Rusty held out. I felt as though she enjoyed taking it away from me.

My history with Rusty induced paranoia. She always seemed ready to lock me up. She had actually smirked at me behind George's back. Did she think I was competing with her for George? Was I competing with her for George? Could I compete with someone who was gorgeous, physically fit, and understood his profession after I split us up because I didn't want him to become a cop? Had he confided in her? What did Jack say? Just because you're paranoid doesn't mean they aren't out to get you. I hoped there was nothing weird on my phone.

"I'll call and let you know when you can pick it up." George handed me his notebook and pen. "Login ID, passcode, password. Whatever I need to get into your phone, please."

I would have teased him about delivering it, but Rusty was watching us both. I took the pen and wrote down my passcode. Good thing I hadn't used *GorgeousGeorge* as a password on any of my apps.

"I'm sure I don't have to tell you this, but you should change your passcode when you get your phone back."

When they left, I called Tina on my landline to tell her about Frank's visit, his threat, and his complaint to the police. I felt bereft without my cell. No looking things up as I thought of them. No quick snaps of Thor being cute. No speakerphone.

"I'm really surprised that he'd want to involve the police. I wonder what he thinks we gave you? Can you come over to the office and bring everything Aunt Gen gave you? I'll have a look at it to see if there's anything there he might want."

Not that I didn't trust her, but I wanted copies. Without my phone, I had to make copies on my printer. I left the copies on there and took the originals with me.

A closed sign was taped to the window when I arrived. DNA genealogy companies weren't the sort to hang open or closed signs out, but she had said to meet her there, so I tried the door, and it gave way. I entered slowly. The lights in the waiting room were dim.

"Tina? It's Cass," I called out.

Much to my relief, her head popped out of the office at the end of the hall. "Hi, Cass. Be right with you."

I heard her voice and the voice of a man that sounded vaguely familiar.

The office door opened again. Tina and Sebastian Kane walked down the hall toward me.

"Hi, Cass. Do you know Sebastian Kane? He's handling my aunt's will and estate." She looked at him. "And now my own will."

"Of course. We met last year."

I held out my hand. His was warm and reassuring, as was his smile. Tall and slim with graying temples, every time I met him, he projected an air of confidence and caring, which is why I'd felt so secure hiring him to defend a friend last Christmas. He was the sort of man who made you feel as though he completely understood you and your situation and could handle anything.

"Nice to see you again, Cass." He shook my hand and then turned back to Tina. "Tina, I'll get back to you this afternoon. Bye now." He pulled the door shut behind him.

Tina turned the lock. "I'm not expecting anyone else, and to be honest, I'm a bit jumpy when I'm here alone. Ever since Aunt Gen…" She wiped away a tear. "C'mon back to the office."

The part of the office suite I could see was tastefully decorated in shades of gray, green, and pale blue with rust accents. A few bronze pieces adorned the shelving, acting as bookends for the various genealogy tomes. I thought that was a nice touch, given that most research was done online these days.

Tina led me into Gen's office but left the door cracked. She caught my eye. "Sorry again. I want to be able to hear if anything happens anywhere in the office."

"I understand completely. My first summer here, an exsanguinated body turned up on the beach by my bungalow. Two little holes over the jugular. Made it hard to sleep at night."

She put her hand to the side of her neck. "I remember that. He was the other bookstore owner, right?"

"That's right. His daughter Mia is a partner in CaRiMia."

She nodded as I talked. "Yes, I read about your

company name on your site." She shuffled a few papers and pulled one out of the stack. "Sebastian has been handling legal matters for the company for a while. He and Aunt Gen were friends. Although he's not an estate lawyer, he'll be taking care of this, too. It's not complicated. Aunt Gen never married and never had kids. She said I was her heir, but you never really know. Frank…" She shook her head. "Sebastian confirmed it and agreed with what you told me. She had a will because he let her know that California takes a chunk of change if you die intestate." She smiled sadly. "He said I should make one right away for the same reason." Her voice quavered. "I'm not married, and I don't have kids." She grabbed a tissue. "Pardon me."

"Of course. I can come back later."

She shook her head. "No, I asked you to come over. Did you bring the papers?"

I handed her the folder.

Looking down, she flipped through the sheets. "Sebastian said Aunt Gen never had any plans to give the company to Frank. He lied."

"I wonder what made him so angry? What is he looking for?"

She looked up. "There's nothing in these papers that he couldn't pull out of the filing cabinet here or download from our server." She bit her lower lip. "I wonder what he thought she'd given you? Here." She handed the folder back to me.

"No idea."

I couldn't ask this woman for a check right now. "What are you planning to do?"

"I want to keep busy. We have a number of clients. I've been fielding calls from them all day. Some of their general questions we could answer by getting that website up." She pulled an envelope out of the heap. "Here you go. I believe that's the amount you and my aunt agreed upon?"

I pulled the check out. "Perfect. Thanks. I know there will now need to be some changes. A memorial to your aunt?"

She nodded and handed me a sheet of paper. "I've started a list. It's not a complete list, but at least it's a start. Have a look at it and tell me what you think."

I glanced over her list. She wanted to keep the basic design but add a memorial page to her aunt. This addition would focus on how important our ancestors are to us and that we should all gather family information and stories while our loved ones are still with us.

"What about the name of your company? Are you going to change it?"

"She called it Genevieve Genealogy, not Genevieve's Genealogy, so I thought I'd keep it. I like the intertwined Gs as the logo with the overlaid double helix. It's distinctive. Tina's Genealogy or Wright's Genealogy." She shook her head and stuck out the tip of her tongue. "No pizzazz."

I smiled. "I think you're right." I stood. "I'll bring the contract over at your convenience, and we'll get to work."

"One more thing." She shuffled the piles on her desk and pulled out a large manila envelope. "I found this when I went through Aunt Gen's current inbox. It has your name on it. I think this is the information for the estate pages portion of the website. Did Gen go over it with you?" She held the fat envelope out to me.

I took it from her. It was quite heavy and a bit lumpy. "The Richmond estate? Yes, it's to be password protected. A competition of sorts."

Tina nodded. "Yes. Frank's overseeing the contingent of relatives that, I believe, have already arrived in town. Aunt Gen ran the DNA and did the background checks before—" Tina burst into tears and grabbed a tissue. "I'm so sorry. This keeps happening to me. Out of the blue. A wave of sadness." She wiped her eyes.

"You're still working with Frank?" That surprised me although this would be a lot of work for one person.

She nodded. "Until something changes legally. Besides, I need his help. This estate guardianship competition, for lack of a better term, is really complicated. That's part of the reason I've practically moved in here. There's so much to do. Gen…" She cried again.

"I understand. I'll get out of your hair now. I can call you if I have questions." I started toward the door and then turned back. "Did you want to lock the door behind me again?"

"Given Frank's temper and unpredictability, yes. Absolutely." She got up and walked to the door as I stepped out.

I turned toward my car and heard the lock click into place. With Frank's temper, Tina had said. That made me wonder why he was handling the DNA relatives instead of Tina. Perhaps her bursts of grief were the reason. She seemed on the edge of a breakdown. Handling the day-to-day needs of a bunch of competitive people was probably more than she wanted to deal with while grieving the loss of her aunt.

I was almost home when I remembered that I couldn't deposit the check with my phone app. I turned around and headed for the bank drive-through. At least I no longer had to hassle with deposit slips.

At home, I tossed the manila envelope on the table and used the landline to call Ricardo.

"Ricardo! When you get this message, check your bank balance. Tina gave us an advance. I know it's not that much yet, but we also have the distillery proposal. Jack and Gillian will be here any minute. I'll get back to soliciting business next week after they leave."

I ended the call as a crash shook my front door and resounded through my small house. Fearful of what I might find and mindful of Frank's attitude toward me, I grabbed a steak knife, ran to the door, and flung it open.

My brother Jack sprawled on my porch, surrounded by pieces of a foam cooler and cans of beer, a few of which had sprung little amber geysers.

He looked up. "Are you going to add insult to injury by stabbing me with that?"

"I might if you damaged my porch. Seriously, are you all right?"

Gillian closed the car door and strolled over. "Oh, he will be after he stops mourning the lost brews." She struggled to control her laughter.

Jack shot her a dirty look as he sat up. "I need a shower."

"Go on in." I looked around. "I'll clean this up. Then I have so much to tell you."

Jack stared up at me. "You haven't found another body, have you?"

Chapter 6

"I only find them so that you'll have something to do when you visit."

Jack snorted. "What's for dinner or are we going out?"

"I have too much to tell you, and I'd have to keep repeating myself in a crowded restaurant. Let's order pizza from Clem's Clam Shack. But first, go clean up." I made a shooing gesture with my hands.

He grabbed the doorframe and hauled himself up. Then Jack raised an eyebrow. "I saw the news story. I'm inclined to take Thor back with us if you're mistreating him." He dusted bits of foam off his jeans.

I picked up some of the beer cans. "You can't. Your landlord will throw you out, and more importantly, you'd be depriving your favorite ghost of her transportation."

He opened his mouth to retort.

"Go! Or I'll make you clean up your own mess."

Jack scooted down the hall and into the bathroom.

I carried the intact cans into the kitchen, gathered up towels and a garbage bag, and headed back to the porch.

Gillian picked her way gingerly through the wreckage. "I'll send him out for the suitcases." She stopped and snapped her fingers. "He's going to need something to wear after his shower although…" She grinned wickedly.

"Gillian!"

She went back, unlocked the car, got the suitcases, and carried them to the back bedroom.

I cleaned up the mess and dragged the garbage bag to the trash. I was washing my hands when a ghostly cough echoed through my bungalow. So, I left the kitchen and saw the rear half of Doris sticking out of the front door with her legs dangling two feet from the ground.

"Doris? Are you all right?" I frowned and pursed my lips. "Can I help? Pull you out?"

Doris popped back into the room like the cork from a bottle of champagne. "Yeah! Like you could grab hold of my ethereal body."

"Sorry, what was I thinking? Oh, yeah. That you were stuck."

She smirked and then grew serious. "There's a guy with a suitcase walking toward the house."

"What, now?" Then Doris' words registered. "Suitcase?" I went to the window and pulled back the curtains. "Phil!"

Jack, freshly showered, joined me. "Phil?"

I looked at Jack.

"Don't look at me. I'm thinking Gillian and I need a little walk before dinner. Gillian!"

"You don't have to ask me twice. See you later!" And they were out the back door.

"Cowards!" I yelled after them.

"Your ex?" Doris said.

"What is he doing here?"

"Judging by the suitcase, moving in."

"Oh, hell no!"

Doris went all hands-on-hips."I didn't know you knew how to swear."

"Extreme circumstances. I have to think." I jumped at the knock on the door.

Doris raised an eyebrow. "Hate to break it to you, but you're out of time."

Too late to hide. I sighed and opened the door.

"Well, well, well. Look what the cat dragged in." I blocked the door.

Phil held up a hand as if warding me off. "You have every right to be angry."

"Ya think?" I crossed my arms and looked around him to the street. "Where's whatzy doodle?"

"Not very respectful."

"I have no respect for someone who steals another woman's husband."

"You can't steal something that doesn't belong to you. You can't own a person."

And that attitude summed up all our marital conversations. "Ah, so marriage vows are unimportant. They don't constitute a binding legal agreement? Then why did we have to file for a divorce to dissolve said non-existent legal agreement?"

He sighed, which set my teeth on edge. "There's no need to get snippy. That was always your problem."

I smiled. "No, you were always my problem, but not any longer. You can leave now. Bye-bye." I started to close the door.

He held up a hand. "No. Wait. We got off on the wrong foot."

"We?"

"I. Sorry, my fault. I fell back into old patterns. I want to apologize."

"For what?" This ought to be good.

"Are you going to make me say it?" He tilted his head.

I merely raised an eyebrow.

He closed his eyes. "I'm sorry I cheated on you. There. I said it."

Cheated? What about mistreated? I let it pass. It was something, at least.

He opened his eyes, and in that moment, I understood how he used to manipulate me. Yes, his eyes were soulful like those of a wounded puppy that wanted to be held. But this time I detected a flicker in them that he was assessing my reaction and whether or not his ploy had worked yet again.

I laughed. The expression that flashed through my mind was "the truth shall set you free," but it should be "understanding will set you free." And free I was for the first time in years. All the anger, angst, and fear drained away as if someone had pulled the plug out of the bottom of a tub of dirty water.

Now Phil was the one who frowned.

"Tell you what, Phil, you go put your suitcase back in the car."

He started to protest.

I shook my head. "Jack and Gillian are here, and there's no room for you to stay. There's a lovely B&B called the Moon Coast Inn up the road run by a very nice woman by the name of Natalie Sandoval. I'll give you the details after dinner." I was definitely getting a cup of coffee now, to be followed by something stronger later.

At his hopeful expression, I said, "Yes, you can stay for dinner and tell us all about it. We're ordering pizza. Jack and Gillian went for a walk along the beach. They should be back any moment."

Apparently, my brother wasn't going to completely desert me. They returned, laughing and carrying Las Lunas reusable shopping bags.

While Phil returned his suitcase to his car, I made a cup of coffee and headed back to the front door. As Jack and Gillian reached the yard, Jack put a finger to his lips and winked at me. What was he up to?

He stopped so short that Gillian nearly ran into him. "You!" He pointed at Phil.

I knew my baby brother was enjoying this little opportunity for drama, but I stepped into the breach before it could go too far. "Jack, you remember Phil, don't you? He stopped by to say hello." I gave him a moment to digest that before dropping the next tidbit. "And he's staying for dinner."

Jack's mouth opened and shut like a beached fish gasping for air.

Gillian, always quick on the uptake, lifted a bag she was carrying to shoulder height. "I think we bought enough peas from the farm up the road for all of us."

"Excellent addition to our dinner *tomorrow* night." I took the bag from her. "Jack, why don't you order the pizza?" I led the way into the house. "I need a gin and tonic."

I went into the kitchen with the bag, set it on the trestle table, and leaned on the kitchen counter for a few moments, staring blankly out the window. My neighbor Dave's house remained empty. He must still be traveling on his inheritance. I felt more isolated down at the end of the road when he wasn't around. I smiled, remembering him knocking at my back door and scrounging food when he wasn't out surfing. Then I realized that Phil wouldn't vanish in a puff of wishful thinking. So I took a deep breath, cranked up a smile, and went back out to join my guests, invited and uninvited.

I served coffee with fruit tartlets from the Bonne Vie Bakery after we finished dinner, in the hope of sobering Phil up. I wasn't actually sure he was drunk, but he had consumed more alcohol than I could handle.

His conversational gambits ranged from how noisy the ocean was, to Maisie's evil shenanigans, to how no one cared about him despite how wonderful he was to everyone. I suspected Jack of plying him with liquor to loosen him up. But I wanted Phil sober enough to drive to Moon Coast Inn.

Phil leaned back in his chair and raised his cup toward me. "Here's to you, old girl." He sipped and set the cup back in its saucer. "Cute little cottage. You'll have to ask your landlord to spruce the place up a bit."

It was a natural assumption on his part given that I hadn't shared any aspect of my life with him since I'd left. We'd only been communicating through lawyers, and he had a pretty accurate idea of the cost of coastal real estate and my own resources, given that I hadn't hidden any money from him the way he had from me.

I had no wish to inform him of anything personal now.

I nodded. "I'll do that. Now, what brings you to my humble abode?"

We all stared at him.

"Can't a guy visit the woman he shared so much of his life with?"

I hadn't meant to snort. It just came out. Jack

laughed. Gillian smiled behind her napkin.

Phil sat up straight. "Haven't you had enough of this? Don't you think it's about time you came home?" He scanned the room. "You can't be comfortable here in this drafty old house."

A sound like an irritated sigh echoed through the house.

Phil started. "You can even hear the wind through the walls. I'll bet it's not insulated properly. Your pipes will freeze, and your heating bill will go through the roof."

I agreed with Doris' sentiment. "Why are you really here? What happened to your girlfriend Matzoh?"

"Maisie."

"Who names their child after corn?"

"It's an old family name."

"As I said."

He ignored that and stared down into his coffee cup, the bravado the alcohol had given him briefly evaporated like the false courage it was. "She left me."

I heard him, but he'd mumbled and I couldn't resist heckling him. "What now? I couldn't hear you."

He glared at me but spoke up. "She left me."

I pursed my lips and nodded my head. I knew I was being overly dramatic, but I couldn't help myself. He'd put me through so much hell when we were living together.

"So, now second best, which I believe is what you called me, is good enough, is it?"

"Now, Cass—"

"You're back to play 'happy families' as they call it on British television."

Gillian rose to clear the table.

"Cass—"

I picked up the butter knife, turning it in my hand.

Chapter 7

"Cass!"

Jack reached over and took the knife away from me. "Phil, perhaps it's time…"

"Uh, yes." Phil wiped his mouth and pushed back from the table. "Don't worry about directions to the B&B. I'll find it." He left quickly.

Gillian came back from the kitchen and sat on the other side of me. "Are you all right?"

I tried to smile, but it was a crooked one, reflecting my mixed feelings. "Yes, oddly, I'm fine. I'm trying to figure out why I stayed married so long."

Gillian glanced at Jack, and her mouth twisted into a smirk.

"Hey! What?"

Her face relaxed into an affectionate smile. Her half-closed eyes contemplated him under her long lashes. "I guess you're worth the hassle."

Maybe he realized that it wasn't the moment for a clever quip. Jack rose, pulled Gillian into his arms, and gently kissed her. When she kissed him back equally tenderly, I had to look away and acknowledge to myself that my marriage had never had this…whatever this was. I had such mixed emotions seeing Phil again, but now I understood that there was no question of going back. That insight drained the anger I'd felt. It wasn't so much moving on as moving beyond.

I had work to do.

****

By the time Jack and Gillian woke up the next day, I had Tina's contract ready to go. I now had two to drop off. Business was picking up.

"There's coffee. I'll be back very soon to explain."

Tina had called to say that she wanted to get the contract signed quickly because Frank had implied that there was more to his contract and hiring conditions than she knew, and her Aunt Gen might have been meticulous about the DNA and genealogy but not so hot with more mundane paperwork.

I went through the locked door routine again with Tina, and she signed, copied, and locked the contract away.

"You know, we could have done this electronically," I said.

She shook her head. "I don't trust it. I don't trust that Frank can't tamper with those electronic files. You don't know... I had another reason for wanting you to come here. I found one more thing that Aunt Gen had. Here." She thrust a flash drive into my hand. "See what you can find on this."

I turned it over in my hand before shoving it into my jeans pocket. "Have you looked at it?"

She shook her head and started to speak when someone unlocked the front door.

"Who has a key besides you?"

"Frank!" She grabbed my arm. "You should leave. You can go out the back," she whispered. "That door will automatically lock behind you."

I thought about standing my ground, but she was clearly frightened. I would be in his line of sight briefly as I crossed the hall, but it was a risk I'd have to take.

"Bye." I headed for the red EXIT sign.

"Hey, you! Stop!"

I kept going and didn't look back.

Tina stepped into the hall and yelled at him, "What do you think you're doing?"

"What the hell is she doing here?"

"None of your business."

"This is MY business!"

"In your dreams. You're fired!"

"You can't fire me!"

The door slammed behind me. My heart raced as I ran to my car and drove north to drop off the second contract at the distillery. I hoped it would be less dramatic.

I paused in the distillery parking lot to call George and tell him about the scene between Tina and Frank but remembered that I didn't have my cell. I'd call him from home to see if I could get it back.

I grabbed the contract, locked the car, and went in.

****

A furious message from Frank awaited me at home. I played back the landline voicemail.

"Stay away from Tina and my company!"

"Unhappy customer?" Jack asked.

"You could say that. The dead woman was our customer. Now her niece and her employee are fighting for control of the company."

"Judging by the male voice on the answering machine, that was not the niece who's angry with you."

"Nope. That guy has already threatened me and made a complaint about me with the police."

"How is good old George?"

"Barely speaking to me, and he has my cell phone."

"Why does he have your cell?"

"I recorded Frank's threats."

"You do realize that he can make a copy of your phone, scroll through your texts, see who you've called."

"Good luck to him sorting all that out." Then I remembered that I'd recorded a few thoughts about George. That won't be good if he listens to them. Was I weird for doing that? Uh oh. What pictures had I taken?

"If he does, that would put the last nail in the coffin of our relationship."

Or if Rusty listens to them. I had a bad feeling.

"Jack, I have no idea what's on my phone. Pictures might be strange. I take pictures of waves. Looking at the contents of my phone might be like rummaging through my junk drawer."

"Relationship not going well?" Gillian asked, coming into the kitchen.

Her wet hair told me she'd just showered.

I shook my head. "He seems to have pulled away. He was almost hostile after this dead body." I thought back and wondered if I was being overly sensitive.

"Can you blame him?"

"Yes, I can. He should trust me."

"Has he been able to trust you in the past?"

I should know better than to be totally honest with a psychologist, but her comment stung. "No."

"Well?"

I sighed. "Let me guess. I should tell him how I feel."

Gillian poured herself a cup of coffee. "See? You

do know what to do." She smiled at me over the rim of her cup.

The timer on my oven dinged.

"Saved by the bell," I said.

Gillian took a cinnamon-topped coffee cake out of the oven and set it on a trivet to cool. "Hope you don't mind. It's your recipe."

"I'm salivating already. I do have a bit of work I need to do today, and I need to gather up decorations for the St. Patrick's Day dinner, which, by the way, is morphing into an Irish party that includes St. Brigid."

"That's a new twist," Gillian said. "But not an unwelcome one. Sometimes we get into tired grooves during the holidays."

"It's because Samantha's off on a new tangent. Men are out; women are in."

"Works for me." Gillian took another sip.

Jack rolled his eyes. "Men are half the human race."

"Women have been saying that for a hundred years." She arched an eyebrow. "And look where it didn't get us."

"She's moved out on Brendan. Dani... Oh, you haven't met her yet. Anyway, Dani thinks Brendan hurt her feelings," I said.

"Must have been a major faux pas," he said. "To move out of that house. Really dwarfs yours, Cass."

"You're positively clueless," Gillian said.

I took a square of coffee cake and left them to their argument while I got to work on the sites that needed updating for sales. Mailing list notices went out automatically. Those who'd signed up for text messages would receive them today.

When I finished the daily work, I turned to the ghost hop information the distillery had provided. After free handing some layouts, I researched local hauntings and national paranormal events and groups.

I jumped when I felt a hand on my shoulder.

"It's just me. What are you looking at?" Jack leaned over my shoulder. "More ghosts? Looking for friends for Doris? I don't think she likes Phil. She didn't put in much of an appearance last night."

"I don't." Doris materialized. "But that's not why I wasn't around. He's the kind who would try to make money off my existence."

"Is that bad?" Jack asked. "You said you needed money, Cass."

I quickly saved my work on the computer. Doris had a habit of making electronics go haywire. Sure enough, she stuck a hand through my laptop and scattered pixels everywhere.

"Seriously?"

"You're not thinking about going with that clown, are you?" she said.

I shut the laptop. "No, but you're making me have second thoughts."

"Ladies." Jack backed away, then headed for the kitchen and the coffee cake.

"I was a bit surprised you didn't try to scare him out of here."

"I thought about it."

"What held you back?"

Doris faded a little. "I don't know." Her voice took on a tinny quality.

"It's over. I'm not going anywhere. You don't have to worry about him, but it might be a good idea to avoid him. I don't trust him, and I don't know what he'd do if he saw you. Can't think it would be good, though."

Doris vanished in a spray of bubbles.

Returning with a plate of coffee cake and a mug, Jack yawned. "That was new." He sat next to me and perused the sketches I'd made.

I'd lost my train of thought, so I made myself another cup of coffee and took a second piece of coffee cake.

We sat at the dining room table, munching.

"I like these drawings. Maybe Gillian and I can come back for the ghost hop. Sounds like fun."

"I know. I'm thinking of going, also. Why don't you guys tentatively plan on it? Block some time on your work calendar?"

"I'll mention it to Gillian. So, what do you have planned for this Irish dinner Friday?"

I licked the cinnamon off my fingers. "For food, I was thinking potatoes, cabbage, and corned beef. Maybe soda bread?"

"Sounds good. You'd better start inviting people, or they'll make other plans. Who're you thinking of? George?"

"Don't know yet. Maybe. The new professor Dani Boyd. Ricardo and Mia. I was thinking about Brendan and Samantha. Not sure if Phil will still be here."

"How many people can you fit in here?" Jack gazed around, doing mental calculations.

"I have two tables. This table will hold six. The gate leg one in the bedroom I'm using for storage will sit four, so we should aim for no more than ten."

"You're already at eleven with George."

"Not sure I should invite George if Phil is still here.

Not at all sure I want them to even meet."

"Lots of luck avoiding that."

"I know."

"Anyone other than Phil joining us for dinner tonight?"

"What makes you think I'm inviting him tonight?"

"What makes *you* think he won't just turn up?"

"Good point. Guess I'd better quit procrastinating, make up my mind, organize the rest of the week, and actually invite people. I could use a leprechaun about now or an elf or two. I'm running out of time."

"Be careful what you wish for."

I paused. "You know, around here anything's possible."

Gillian joined us. "Did I hear you planning a guest list for Friday's dinner? Hope we're on it."

"Without a doubt. Have some coffee cake. I'll grab my notepad."

Gillian carried what was left of the coffee cake out to the table and cut a piece. "How about Ricardo and Mia? I'd love to see them again."

"Brendan and Samantha," Jack ventured.

"That could be tricky. As I just said, Ricardo told me they've split. We can invite them all and see what happens. Bear in mind that they might not accept. Samantha fired Ricardo."

That stunned them both into silence.

"Today, I have to put some time in on the genealogy gig. I really have to get some work done before Gen's, sorry, Tina's assistant Frank pulls a fast one. You heard the message, Jack. He's trying to stop us for some reason."

"Sounds serious."

"I'll find out as soon as I deliver on Monday. Can you guys entertain yourselves for a few hours while I pore through this data?" I tapped the manila envelope and held up the flash drive Tina had given me. "Think about what you'd like at the party. There are some notes on the coffee table. I had a spurt of inspiration."

"Sure thing." Jack got up. "We'll check in around noon."

"Let us know if we can help." Gillian carried the dishes out to the kitchen.

I had a peek at the flash drive. Tina had shared a great deal of information. I uploaded all the files to the cloud so that I could reach them on all my devices. I loved the freedom of working on my tablet while swinging on the front porch, with ocean breezes cooling me in the summer.

She'd included some client files from those who'd given permission to use their testimonials. I extracted some of the services that she provided, along with quotes from clients who'd given feedback. However, I noticed that she'd also included information on clients who hadn't filed permission slips. Probably an oversight on her part. A bulk download. Perhaps that was why Frank had objected. He needn't have worried. I might get ideas from some of this information, but I wouldn't expose any client data. CaRiMia prided itself on confidentiality.

Something about a cat caught my eye. I'd never particularly liked cats until my baby brother had given me his cat Thor. Now, I was fascinated by them. I sat up straighter and read.

This was related to the password protected area of the website. Gen had wanted a client portal. I reached for the manila envelope and dumped its contents on the table. Yes. Gen's current big project... I corrected myself. Tina's project was the Richmond estate. A woman had left her estate to her cat. Said estate was to be controlled by the cat's caretaker. A rather big estate. This was the second time in the history of this family that the estate had been left to a cat. This was the project Frank was in charge of. I'd better familiarize myself with the details.

The first time, the old woman's daughter, who lived with her, was appointed guardian of the cat for its life, but she would lose the entire estate if the cat went missing, died accidentally, or died from unnatural causes. Now there was a motive for murder if ever there was one. But the daughter married and had a daughter named Sophia who apparently was fine with the setup, was a cat lover herself, and inherited the guardianship.

However, she never married, and the cat lived to twenty and died in its sleep. Sophia died a few months ago. She'd had a long succession of cats but no husband or children. Her will left the estate to her current cat, Sissy. She'd also had Missy and Hissy. I sensed a pattern. The name Hissy conjured interesting images. At least, it wasn't Pissy.

I scanned back through the pile. The original cat was named Prissy. No way. I'd almost forgotten Mina's request to find out what Prissy the Spirit Cat wanted.

How did genealogy fit into this story? I poked around for more data. Gen had been tracking down DNA relatives in the search for an acceptable guardian for the cat, the original choice having been found wanting.

I went back to the files on the flash drive, scrolled,

and found a link to a spreadsheet. It contained names, relationships, DNA relationship results, addresses, phone numbers, and email addresses. I froze. A couple of names caught my eye: Frank Wright and Dani Boyd. I was definitely inviting her to our St. Patrick's dinner celebration.

I was torn between poking around more and creating the new website for Tina. Responsibility and practicality—and the need for a paycheck—won out in the end. I created local and cloud directories for copies of the files I was interested in reading later, those for the portal, and those for the public website but spent the rest of the morning roughing out the public site.

I was ready for lunch when Jack and Gillian returned, bright-eyed and apple-cheeked from their walk.

"We ran into Phil in town. He was having coffee with two women. He introduced us. Honey, do you remember their names? They're all staying at the B&B. The women are in town to take DNA tests for your client. Something about proving they're related to a recently deceased woman."

I leaned back in my chair, and my mouth fell open. I closed it quickly. Having Phil suddenly tied into my job, my source of income—something he knew nothing about—was highly uncomfortable.

"Alice Wembley and Emily Beaton." Gillian frowned. "Cass, are you all right?"

I swallowed. I remembered their names from the papers I'd looked through this morning. My mouth was dry. I needed to know how much he knew.

"I think it would be charitable to invite Phil over for dinner tomorrow."

Jack and Gillian stared at me and then looked at each other. I might have been reading too much into their expressions, but it looked as though they were ready to have me hospitalized for observation.

I stood. "Seriously. It would be downright rude not to invite him."

Not to mention that he might be easier to pump for information than anyone else I knew who was involved. Once he got going, it might be hard to shut him up.

One side of Jack's mouth screwed up, and his eyes narrowed. "All right. Give. What are you up to?"

I widened my eyes to try to look innocent, but I'm no actor. "I just—"

"Oh, don't give me that! I'm your brother. Be straight with us."

They'd be gone in a few days. There was no point in trying to keep this from them, and they had been helpful in the past.

"Something *is* going on, but I'm not sure what. Tina gave me some files for Genevieve Genealogy. They contained information about some DNA testing of relatives of an elderly woman who died, leaving everything to her cat."

I caught the look that passed between them.

"See what I mean? We have to find out what Phil discovered out at Natalie's."

"Cass, you can't get involved. I know you. You think the old lady's death is another murder. Some people just plain die. We won't be here to look out for you, and you can't trust Phil."

"I know, but we need the job. We have to protect our client's best interests. Also, I think people aren't aware of murders all around them. I doubt that many

69

murderers are caught. Not the clever ones, in any case. Autopsies are much rarer these days. Too expensive. If it looks like an accident or natural causes, most murders would be ignored. Not on purpose but because they'd be nearly invisible in the glut of death."

Jack started to speak, stopped, opened his mouth, and then closed it. His cheeks puffed out, and his face reddened. He exhaled hard. "All right, but call Mia and Ricardo over here and let them in on the whole thing. Let's see if they think it's worth the risk. It is their company, too."

I moved my hands in a downward motion that I hoped was a calming gesture. "I will, but you need to sit down and do some deep breathing. This isn't good for your blood pressure."

He sat. "I only want *you* to continue to have blood pressure."

"No one's going to try to hurt me." I dismissed the thought of Frank's threat and went to pull out my cell phone before I remembered that George still had it. "But you're right. We can't invite Ricardo and Mia and not let them in on what's going on."

"You could consider inviting George, too," Gillian said.

"He won't come."

"Then there's no harm inviting him, is there?"

"I'll invite him to the party, but we need to talk to Mia and Ricardo as soon as possible without anyone else around."

Chapter 8

Ricardo and Mia were all in, but my calls to Brendan and Samantha were harder. I had to tell each that the other was also invited, which meant I now had two tentative acceptances. I'd have to plan for eleven at the dinner party, in any case, but I would prefer to have them here as a buffer. Phil would be a wildcard.

"I hate to bring it up again." Jack hesitated. "What about George?"

I winced. I knew he would bring it up again. "Sore subject. I doubt that he'd expect an invitation. Not now."

"I'm sorry," Gillian said. "I know how you feel about him."

"Sometimes you can't go home again. We're very different people from the college kids who fell in love a lot of years ago."

"I've seen the recent sparks," Jack said. "But it might not be a great idea to have him at dinner with Phil. The party is a different matter. There are enough people that we can keep them at separate tables."

"Yeah, I'd rather err on the side of caution. If he were to get to know Phil, he'd question my taste and my sanity."

Jack laughed. "Kidding aside, we left you alone this morning to study this stuff from Tina. Then you drop a bomb. Now you have to fill us in. What's the deal with the cat and the DNA?"

"I printed out some of it. Can you grab it from the printer in your bedroom?"

Jack hopped up and ran back to get it. He was reading both the originals I had left when I'd copied the first files and the ones from the flash drive that I'd just printed when he returned. "Do us a favor and don't hit print in the middle of the night."

"No problem. I didn't have room for it out here, and I have too much stuff in the other bedroom to find a plug easily."

"This is interesting. It's a family thing. Quite matrilineal. Her grandmother left a small fortune to a cat named Prissy in the Thirties."

Mina's spirit cat. I hadn't mentioned her request to them. Perhaps tonight.

He continued, "That time with the proviso that her daughter should look after the cat and inherit when the cat died. The cat didn't live long, but then neither did the daughter, whose own daughter inherited in her turn, didn't have a daughter to leave it all to and, as a result, probably saved her own life but now has left it all to another cat, Missy. Not much imagination with the names."

I thought I heard a growl.

Gillian said, "I'm not sure I followed all that."

Jack handed her the printout. "Missy seems to be the cat for which they're currently seeking a caretaker."

Gillian looked it over. "While this is fascinating, I'm not sure that it has anything to do with Gen's murder."

"It's odd that she gets murdered while…"

"While what?"

I started to say, 'while investigating a murder.' But she wasn't, was she? Why did my subconscious go there? When I thought about it, the old lady had died from a variety of natural causes.

"Her death certificate said renal failure, but her DNA analysis listed a whole mess of medical conditions, which just meant that ultimately, her heart stopped. On the other hand, there were a number of things that could cause kidney failure, such as too much aspirin. Or is that liver failure? My brain always goes to the dark side, and I have no idea why."

"Maybe because you've been in the middle of murder since you bought this place."

"Not really. People die all the time. As I said, I'm of the opinion that most murders go completely unnoticed. For example, the old lady with the cat had slipped into a coma, so if she'd taken too many or was forced to take too many painkillers, who would know? Or opiates? No one's going to do an autopsy when the patient has been under recent medical care, unless a family member is willing to pay for it, when it so clearly looks like natural causes. Not to mention that you'd have to have a designated family member request one, and that's what Gen was looking for."

"Have you thought about therapy?" Jack smirked.

"Do you want to be invited back to my little beach bungalow?"

"Point taken. But it is a big legal case, and Gen was doing the lion's share of the work of looking for next of kin. Who stands to gain with her gone?"

"Tina," Gillian said.

"Frank might," I added. "He said Gen had promised him the business, or at the very least, he had reason to expect that Tina would let him run the business. That would have enhanced his reputation. Is there such a thing as a forensic genealogist?"

"Beats me," Jack said.

"Yes, there are. Don't you two watch television? I hear that testifying in legal cases can be quite lucrative," Gillian said.

"Ah, filthy lucre as motive for murder… again." I shook my head.

"It's one of five main reasons along with lust, envy…no, wait, those are the seven deadly sins. I meant love, jealousy, ambition, anger, filthy lucre…Yeah, there's some overlap with the deadly sins. Funny that," Jack said.

"You are such a cynic!" Gillian said. "How does it go? Money is the root of all evil?"

I frowned. "That's a misquote. If I remember correctly, it's the love of money that's the root of all evil."

"Greed," Jack said. "Plain and simple."

"You could be right." I nodded. "Jack? I really have to finish up the ghost hop stuff, but we're going to need groceries. We had pizza last night. Ricardo and Mia are going to come tonight to discuss all this. And I was wondering…"

"Uh-oh. Here it comes."

Gillian looked up from petting Thor.

"I think we should invite Phil for dinner tomorrow night, telling him he's on his own tonight."

"What?"

"He can invite one of the women from the inn out to dinner tonight."

"Why?"

"I want to know more about why he's here."

"Isn't it obvious?"

"And what he's found out about the DNA relatives."

"Again, why?"

"I've been thinking that somehow they tie in."

Jack frowned. "Tie in to what? Not the ghost hop?"

Gillian quit petting Thor, and he wandered off. "No, darling. The murder."

"Why would they bump off the woman who'd sought them out and put them in line for a lucrative inheritance?"

I shook my head. "I'm not saying they're suspects, but their case was the one Gen was working on when she was murdered. Something to hide, maybe?"

Jack rubbed his neck. "Do we have to have dinner with Phil two nights in a row?"

"The more I think about it, getting info out of him in a crowd of people might prove too hard. You can pump him for information tomorrow night, Jack. Enjoy yourself. Make it a game. Do one of your spreadsheets."

"You're bored, aren't you, Sis?"

"Not bored. Just need to take my mind off certain things."

"Certain tall, dark, handsome, and Hawaiian things?" He smirked.

I sighed. I had no idea where I stood with George, and it was driving me nuts. I thought everything was going great after Christmas. New Year's. Then nothing. Talk about dry January! Valentine's day brought a card and flowers, but George seemed distant and, if not cold, certainly chilly.

"Maybe."

"Okay. Anything for you, Sis."

"Thanks, Jack."

"We'll grab a sandwich while we're out. Want anything?"

"I could eat the leftover pizza."

Jack straightened his six-foot-two frame, widened his eyes, and held out two crossed fingers as if warding off a vampire. "We'll bring you a sandwich!"

Chapter 9

After they left to run errands, I called Phil.

"Who is this?" He sounded grumpy.

"Hi, Phil. This is Cass on my landline."

"Where have you been? I've been calling your mobile all day."

"The police have it."

"The police!"

"It's a long story. Listen, I was calling to invite you to dinner tomorrow night. Just the four of us. The day after is the St. Patrick's dinner, which you're also invited to. Feel free to bring a plus one to the party, but not to dinner tomorrow."

"Can I bring plus two?"

I suppressed a chuckle. He worked fast. "To the party, yes. You've been in my house, so it might be a bit of a tight fit for the party, depending on who shows up."

"No problem. I was calling about tomorrow night. The two women I want to bring to the party are attending some get-together about this DNA thing they're involved with tomorrow night, so the timing works well. You're the only other person I know in town."

"Tomorrow night will be informal, you understand, and it won't be a late night. I have a lot of party prep to do for the following night."

"Do you know enough people to host a party?"

Despite my desire to retort, I didn't really want him to know my business. "I'm living in a small bungalow, but you can always go back to Pleasanton."

Silence.

"Phil?"

His voice was tired. "She changed the locks."

I rolled my lips inward and held them between my teeth in an effort not to laugh. Then I exhaled. When I was under control, I said, "I'm sorry, but how can Maisie change the locks on your house? Don't you have title to the house? As I recall—"

"I put her name on it."

"Ah. Well, I guess she's within her rights to toss you out then. Come along around six tomorrow night, and we can talk over dinner. See you then." I hung up and laughed.

Gotta love karma.

Back to work. I stalked around the first floor, trying to come up with ideas. I'd read through all the materials, but nothing sparked. Ghosts seemed incompatible with the clean, industrial location of the distillery. I was missing something. Who were the ghosts? Surely, they must have an idea beyond clichés like, "the woman in white" or "the evil child."

"Doris!"

When she didn't immediately appear, I walked around, calling for her, until I noticed an eyeball up by the ceiling, which stopped me cold. "Doris? If that isn't you..." I didn't even want to think what it might be. My mind was on ghosts and monsters.

Her body popped into existence around her eyeball and floated to the ground. "I've never heard you call out that way. I wasn't sure what to expect."

I sighed. "I'm stumped. The distillery doesn't seem like a haunted space. I can't envision it, and if I can't see it in my mind, I can't create a campaign around it. You have to help me. Who…what are the ghosts there?"

"Oh, is that all? The way you were screeching…"

I ground my teeth and exhaled. "Doris."

"Yes'm?" She held her hands together primly, one atop the other, tips of the fingers curled around the other fingertips. Doris was a ghost of many moods.

"What ghosts reside at the distillery?"

"Got a pen?"

I took a deep breath, sat, and pulled a notebook and pen over. "Ready."

"Elena died in 1795. Jeremiah died in 1849. William died in 1921. Two dogs. Six cats. I have no ideas how many rabbits and squirrels."

"Squirrels?"

"And thirty mice."

"You're kidding me."

"Do you want me to list the bugs?"

"There are bug ghosts?"

"No. *Now* I'm kidding you."

"Thirty mice. That's bad enough. I'm thrilled that there're no cockroach ghosts."

Doris opened her mouth.

I held up a finger. "Don't start. Tell me about Elena. Does she manifest?"

Doris transformed into a classic, see-through, woman-in-white ghost, moaned, and floated six inches off the ground. Her dark bob grew into long, white hair that hung loose and tangled halfway down her back.

The two touches of color were blood-red lips and glowing yellow eyes.

Incongruously, Doris's voice was normal and chatty when she spoke from that frightening visage. "Elena started out looking like herself and crying a lot when she figured out that she was dead. Died in childbirth as did her son who—*pfft*—went into the light, of course, because he was an innocent. Her revenge was transforming into the kind of ghost her mother used to scare her with when she misbehaved."

"I can work with that." I doodled a rough approximation of the ghost Doris manifested next to her story. "Jeremiah?"

"He found gold and was killed for his claim. His ghost, when he's seen, looks like a scary old man, but he was forty-five when he died." She morphed into a short, whippet-thin, shaggy-looking man in dirty clothes with long hair and a beard. He had the most haunted eyes I've ever seen—pale blue, hooded with a startled expression. "They aged fast in those days."

"He looks lost." I sketched him in broad strokes before Doris could morph again.

"He is. But I think William is your key. I know him. When I've been able to get to the distillery, I've talked to him."

I wondered how she did that while inhabiting a rodent… or my cat. "Bootlegger?"

She nodded.

"Show me."

She transformed into a slightly old-fashioned but very attractive man. Rolled sleeves revealed tattoos on muscled arms. His intelligent face was heart-shaped.

"Does he manifest?"

She shook her head. "He manipulates the others. Stirs them up. The dogs are his."

"What about the cats?"

"Oddly, the cats prefer hanging out with the women."

"Can anyone see these ghosts?"

She shrugged. "A lot of people claim to see them. Thor can see them. We've been there together."

"That's miles up the highway!"

"Open trucks and trailers never seem to notice when a cat hitches a ride."

I couldn't let Jack know that his cat had been hitchhiking. "You've given me an idea for a contest if the management at the distillery will go along with it, and we'll find out if people can really see them."

"Then you need to know that there's one more. No one knows much about her. She doesn't speak, but her energy is overwhelming. I think she's ancient. She's really what everyone feels. When you see someone walk in, stop, shiver, and then look around, that's her. I advise you to stay away from her... particularly at night."

"After what you told me, I'm only going there during daylight!" Then I remembered that the ghost hop was at night.

Jack and Gillian came in, bearing lunch.

"Oh, good. I very nearly devoured your pizza."

Jack thrust a paper sack into my waiting hands.

"Nothing for me?" Doris said, going platinum blonde and slinky à la Marilyn Monroe.

Jack stared.

Gillian nudged him. "Remember what it feels like when she touches you."

Jack shivered. "Forgot for a moment."

Doris laughed and blinked out of our plane of existence.

"Okay, Jack. Did you bring your computer? I'd rather you used yours for our murder spreadsheet. I still have work to do for CaRiMia."

He set his lunch down on the table. "Sure thing. I'll get it." He went down the hall to the bedroom.

"Gillian, Ricardo and Mia will be here tonight. Phil will be joining us for dinner tomorrow night. I'm hoping to get some information from him about the DNA—what do I call them?—contestants? That'll do. They are contesting for the guardianship position. I have a bunch of loose data from Tina. I still haven't come up with a theme. Maybe Ricardo and Mia can help with that. When I work on sites, I like to find binding elements to tie things together. Working with Gen would have been a lot easier. She had a sense about people and relationships. Tina is really fraying around the edges, and Frank has been nothing but hostile. Can you help with pulling dinner together and wrangling Phil tomorrow? Sorry, I know you guys are guests, too."

She smiled and shook her head. "No, we're family, and of course I'll pitch in. The image of wrangling Phil that I saw in my mind for a moment was of him hogtied. But don't worry. I can be subtle."

"I know that. Thanks. I'm really curious about the contestants. It'll be harder to talk to him at the party. That'll be my chance to meet two of the contestants and gather some impressions. Also, turns out that Frank and Dani are listed as DNA relatives. I really wish I could talk to George about Frank. I feel shut out." I thought for a moment. "I need to find out what George and Rusty have concluded about Gen's murder and who might have done it."

"Don't do anything foolish and don't worry about tomorrow night. If I remember rightly, Phil likes Italian, which is easy to pull together and won't conflict with Friday night's Irish theme. You are aware that he needs a woman in his life to take care of him? You aren't falling for it, are you?"

"Not on your life! His shenanigans pulled the curtain back, and I saw the wizard for who he truly is. I think I missed the lifestyle more than Phil."

"But you wouldn't go back for the lifestyle?"

"No," I said with certainty. "Even with the financial ups and downs, this has been more fun than I've had in years."

"Even with the bodies on the beach?"

"Grisly as that part's been, it brought George back into my life… at least for a while."

"Don't give up yet.

"I won't."

Chapter 10

Jack and I spent a couple of hours organizing the information we had so far into two spreadsheets: Jack's murder spreadsheet and another one for the Richmond estate information. I had a strong suspicion that the two were entangled.

I leaned back in my chair. "It's very annoying not to be able to poke George for info. The newscasters don't seem to be following the story anymore. I have a strong desire to be an *agent provocateur*." I wanted to flush the birds from the hedgerows to find out what was going on.

Jack must have read my mind… or the expression on my face.

"Cass! Whatever it is, don't do it."

"Relax! I won't cause any trouble before our dinner tonight with Ricardo and Mia. Let's keep working on the estate spreadsheet. That's the one they need to be briefed on. This should help Ricardo decide which photos to take for that section of the site. We need a focal point that's bigger than the fortunate cat. You should pardon the pun."

Jack stopped typing. "What pun?"

"Fortune and fortunate. The cat's worth a fortune; therefore, the cat's fortunate. Not really a pun, I guess. More a play on words. Were you paying attention to me at all?"

"Nope. I stuck that flash drive into my computer and was reading some of the data. I'm stunned by the detailed information on these participants."

"It didn't occur to me until you said that, but I'll need you to sign a nondisclosure agreement for CaRiMia. Gillian, too."

"No problem."

I opened my laptop and sent two copies to the printer in their bedroom.

A plan took form in my brain. I'd need Doris' help. I put that aside for now to fill Jack in on the distillery ghosts so that he could add them to the information I was giving Ricardo and Mia over dinner.

****

Ricardo and Mia arrived at quarter to five. The weather had turned, and they dripped from the drizzle. We left their umbrellas open on the hearth rug and hung their jackets on the hall tree.

"Come in and get warm," I said. "Dinner's almost ready."

Ricardo went off to the kitchen with Jack and Gillian to get drinks. Mia and I sat in the living room where Gillian brought us cocoa in demitasse cups a few minutes later.

"To warm you up."

Jack turned the fireplace on, and we all took a moment to relax and settle before dinner.

"So much has happened since our last business meeting," I said. "The business is changing, and the tools are improving. Social media blasts and ads could be part of our business. We've focused on small businesses, but they've taken a hit lately. Would we be smart to branch out to individuals and social media?"

"What do you mean, individuals?" Ricardo asked.

"More people work from home and have side hustles. We could scale our services. Also, I finished a mystery right before Jack and Gillian arrived. In the back of the book, the author had a list of sites to follow her on. I loved her book, so I signed up for her newsletter. I immediately got an email with a link to her website where I could download a free short story. I scrolled through and then explored a number of other author sites."

"But aren't there a lot of people doing author websites?" Mia asked.

"I'm thinking of ways to supplement what we're doing. Doesn't have to be authors. We could advertise at freelancers of all sorts. When I was in the candle shop, talking to the owner about her promotional budgeting, I realized that it might be time to add more layers to our services and also a payments hierarchy. Just a thought. Let's have dinner while it's hot and then run through the Richmond estate data and the stuff for the Coastal Ghost Hop."

****

"That was delicious," Mia said. "The ghost hop sounds like something Ricardo and I would like to go to."

"Agreed," Ricardo said. "I'll mockup a few designs. Just a thought, but perhaps they'd be up for having us do a few email campaigns from their ghosts, providing some of their history. I like the quiz idea. That's hilarious about the mouse ghosts."

"Speak for yourself," Mia said.

Ricardo pulled a folded orange sheet of paper out of his pocket and unfolded it on the table, pressing it flat. "Three of my cousins are opening a bike shop. Same story. Not a big budget for advertising, but I gave them a few promo ideas for students and said I'd post some of these flyers on campus. They said we could do an inexpensive website for them."

Mia put her hand on his and leaned forward. "The idea being that they'll grow and it's a potential in to the bike community, which is growing around here. Cutting them a deal could end up being worth it."

"I like it. Another avenue to pursue: hobby and athletic organizations and groups. You don't have to have a store front to need a website and media sources. Can I hang onto this?"

"Sure."

"If we get enough of this type of business, we could offer an internship through Clouston College's marketing program." I made a few notes on my laptop. "I know I've mentioned that you should take the Richmond photos, but I think this new information should help you target the ones we need. We've also gotten great feedback on that augmented college campus tour we did for Clouston. I'd like to work up a formal presentation for other small colleges and private schools. There are a lot of them in California. Maybe Dani would be willing to give us some feedback on such a preso from an academic point of view."

"I can talk to her," Ricardo said.

"I'd like to check out the AI graphics programs that are out there," Mia said. "I think they could be useful for quick versioning of some of Ricardo's designs."

"I like it," I said.

Gillian got up to clear.

Mia started to help, but I stopped her.

"I know you have studying to do. Don't worry about this."

"Thanks. I do have a quiz tomorrow."

I looked out the window. "At least the rain's stopped."

They put on their jackets.

"Thanks for dinner!"

"You're more than welcome. Be careful driving home."

I watched them until they drove away. "Ricardo really looked tired."

"I was tired all through college," Jack said.

"That's because you gamed until all hours and then crammed."

Chapter 11

I beat them both down for breakfast and had time for a little budgeting before Gillian joined me. I hastily shoved my notepad into my junk drawer. "Morning!"

"Morning." Gillian had seen my gesture, opened the drawer, and pulled the notepad out. She nodded as she read the figures. Set the notepad down and looked at me seriously. "We talked last night." She drew a line through the amount they'd spent on shopping for the party.

"I will pay you back."

She shook her head. "No, you won't. This is a gift from us. We come often and eat you out of house and home. We're both working, and it's unfair of us to assume you'll welcome us with open arms if we're always taking and never giving."

"I love having you visit."

"And we love visiting, so we want to help out now and then to maintain our welcome." She bent over and hugged me.

"Thanks. I'm afraid I'm a bit pinched for funds right now, but we do have some new prospects."

"That's great, but you need at least six months of emergency funds set by. From the looks of this budget, you're spending everything you earn."

Jack walked in, yawning and tousle-haired from sleep. "We thought we'd come back over the summer and help with some repairs and painting."

"I'd love that!"

Gillian put the notepad back in the drawer. "Good. That's settled then. We have our menu for tonight. I'm going to owe you some color cartridges for your printer. I printed out a few images of St. Brigid and also some of the goddess Brigid. This is a pencil drawing by a young artist of St. Brigid hanging her cloak on a sunbeam. Unlike St. Patrick, she was actually born in Ireland."

I looked over the printouts. "Her feast day is Imbolc, February 1st, the start of spring on the wheel of the Celtic calendar. We'll have to celebrate it on time next year." I picked up a lopsided straw cross with even legs. "I've seen this before."

"That's St. Brigid's cross. I found those at Connie's Crafts in town. I thought we could hang some up where we don't have shamrocks. Some of these things can be conversation starters. Next year, you might have a craft party on her feast day to make these for your friends' homes."

"Love it! Many of these images look like a nun while others look a bit like Samantha with her flaming red hair."

"St. Brigid was the abbess, the head of a nunnery. The goddess Brigid or Brid is a red-headed woman. I was also struck by the resemblance to Samantha. Oh, and here's a feminist tidbit for Samantha when you talk to her. The initial community was expanded into two: one for nuns and one for monks. The abbess was more powerful than the abbot."

"Are you sure about that?"

Gillian shrugged. "As sure as I can be. Samantha

can research further if she wants. Speaking of research, have you thought about asking Brendan to see if he has any books on Brigid at his shop?"

"Great idea! I'll give him a call."

"Her holiday is also Imbolc."

"Oh, now, that's interesting."

Mia called and sounded hesitant. "Cass, I've gotten a small job with the yarn shop."

"You must have more charisma than I do."

"It's not what you think. I'm taking knitting classes, but it can get costly, so I stopped for a bit. Felicity called to tell me about her new Knit a Gnome class, and when I told her that money was really tight, she said that if I'd design, copy, and post flyers, plus update their website with my design, I could take the class for free. She's even providing the yarn I'd need if I don't already have sufficient. It's not really a job for CaRiMia, but since you talked to them about a contract, it felt like I was going behind your back."

I laughed. "It's really sweet of you to worry about that, but you need to take your opportunities when they're offered to you. I'd feel horrible if you missed out on gnome knitting because of loyalty to me."

"Thanks, Cass. I knew you'd understand. One more thing. If we do decide to work with authors, Felicity is writing a romance. Something to keep in mind. Ricardo's going to help me. Did you know that Prof Boyd is going on that all-day hike through the state park that Frank set up for bonding?"

"I like Dani. I hope she's selected as the conservator of the estate if that's what she wants."

"Her contract at the college is only for a year. Sort of a trial period, I guess. Not sure how that works, but I know she could use the money."

"Enjoy yourselves. We got approval on the materials I took to the distillery, so I'll get started on the ghost hop material."

I thought about Dani. That folklore position seemed doomed to me. There always seemed to be somebody new teaching it. I hoped she'd be okay on the hike. I shook my head. Of course, she would be. She was young, healthy, and a forager.

I'd barely hung up when the phone rang again.

"When are you getting your cell phone back?" Gillian asked.

"That's another call I have to make." I picked up the phone. "Oh, hi, Ricardo."

"Can you take the photos of the hike?"

"I don't know if I'm a good enough photographer to do that."

"We only need some candids to post."

"All right. Send the—Oh, no, I still don't have my cell. Better send it to email. It'll be easier to print out from there. Study hard, but get your sleep, too."

"Come over and I'll lend you a camera."

"Sure thing. See you later."

I hung up. "Looks like I'm going on the hike to take photos for the portal. Ricardo and Mia have midterms and can't go."

"I would say 'have fun,'" Gillian said. "But I know better."

"Frank is the leader for the event." I made a face. "Not my favorite person after he threatened me."

"If he's so against CaRiMia's involvement, why would he let Ricardo go?"

"Self aggrandizement? I don't really know. Maybe

they hit it off." I shrugged. "I'd better see if I can find my suit of armor. I'm only half-joking."

Jack walked out of the kitchen, blowing on his cup of coffee, and dug his pocket knife out of his pocket. "Take this, just in case."

"Do you have any idea how long it would take me to dig out one of these blades? I'd probably get the scissors instead."

"So hold it in your fist and hit him with it. Trust me, it has heft."

I wrapped my fingers around it. "Not bad." I stuffed it into my pocket. "I'm going to run over to Ricardo's to grab some camera equipment. I don't even have my cell to take pictures with. Will you be okay until I return?"

"Of course." Jack took a tentative swig. "We're grownups most of the time."

"Sorry. You'll always be my kid brother." I thought for a moment. "What am I saying? Gillian, you'll keep an eye on him, won't you?"

We both laughed, and Jack's mouth twisted in disgust.

I grabbed the car keys and drove over to Ricardo's.

When I arrived, he was waiting at the door for me. I peered over his shoulder and realized why he wouldn't be inviting me in. Every surface was either covered with paper, food, bottles, or takeout containers.

I took the bag he proffered. "Anything I need to know?"

"There are a couple in there. One is a point and shoot if the others defeat you, but I wrote up some instructions. I'm sorry. But there aren't enough hours in the day."

"I understand. School is more important."

"I don't want to be rude…"

"Leaving now."

I drove home, thinking about how to handle this. I decided business and detached was the only way to deal with Frank.

I passed the office of Genevieve Genealogy on the way home. A tall, silver-haired man let himself into the office. My first thought was Tina's lawyer, Sebastian Kane, but the man's hair seemed too silvery. At least it wasn't Frank.

Back at home, I called Frank and left a voicemail, telling him why I was replacing Ricardo and asking him to use my landline or email if there were any changes in location or time.

I changed into hiking gear, filled a small backpack with items I might need, and moved some of the camera gear into it. I'd be taking my walking sticks, so I needed both hands free. The net pockets on either side of the backpack would provide sufficient space for two bottles of water. I paused and called Dani.

"Hi. Can I ride with you to the hiking spot? Twenty minutes? I'll be ready."

I grabbed a couple of bars, an apple, and made a quick peanut butter and jelly sandwich, which I stashed in a slightly oversized plastic grip seal bag. I could use that to carry out any trash I might have.

I was at the door when she pulled up. I put my sticks and pack in the back and climbed in front next to her. "Good afternoon."

"I certainly hope it will be," she said. "Do you know the park we're going to?"

I'd initially assumed it was the one near my house

that the local vampire cosplayers used, but Frank had provided directions to Tarquin State Park twenty minutes up the road and inland a couple of miles. I wasn't familiar with it. "Not really. I've never been to this one. New experience."

"I wonder what kind of team building activities he's dreamed up?"

"I'm curious about why you'd want to build a team when you'll all be competing with one another."

"My thoughts exactly. And why a hike in a park? A few are older people with arthritis."

"I'll find out tonight how well two of them survived. Emily Beaton and Alice Wembley are coming to my house for dinner. My ex invited them."

She raised an eyebrow. "Those two are on the younger side, which is probably why your ex is flirting with them." She concentrated on finding a parking spot. "Oh, this is nice. A picnic table and composting toilet here by the entrance. Just in case."

"I did bring a roll of camping TP with me."

"You're well prepared."

"Not really. I have to take the pictures for the portal. Ricardo would normally do it, but he has midterms. I assume you're not giving a midterm today."

"No. Tomorrow, actually." She locked the car.

"Sorry," I said. "Guess that was obvious."

We started for the table.

"Good place to meet," she said, looking at her watch. "We're only a few minutes early. Oh." She pointed. "There's Frank now."

He strolled over to us. "Glad you could make it, Dani." His smile at Dani turned into pursed lips for me. "Cass, please don't insert yourself into any of the proceedings, not even to tell people to line up for a shot. Please take candid pictures only and let things play out naturally. I want the bonding process to take place."

I wondered why, given that only one would be left in the end, but nodded obediently.

Soon the others gathered, and Frank handed out paperwork and divided them up into teams.

I tapped him on the arm. "Could I have a set, please?"

"Why?"

"So that I get all the participants' names straight and call all the events by their correct names."

He nodded and reluctantly handed over a set of papers. I scanned them, wishing I had my cell to take a picture to send to Jack. I'd get everyone in the candid snaps. I hung back and followed them down the trails and up the hills. I frequently had company as people who hadn't hiked for years dropped back. I didn't take many pictures until we stopped at our first clearing where I got several good shots of the participants as they broke into groups and started reading the directions.

My mind drifted as the earthy smell of warming soil and the scent of pine wafted through the air. Birds sang in the trees. Sunlight dappled the ground and the wings of the butterflies.

We'd only been walking for half an hour when a man shouted. I snapped back to the present to see Dani frantically dumping stuff out of her pack and breathing rapidly. The red case of her inhaler lay next to her on the ground.

She upended the bag in the dirt.

Chapter 12

Frank yelled, "Everyone, stay here. I don't have reception. I'm going to run back toward the entrance and call for EMTs." He took off.

No one helped her. I ran over toward Dani. Then small groups also headed toward her from paths in the woods.

"Can I help?"

She didn't speak, waved a hand at me, and continued to flick her possessions away. In a few minutes, she found a second inhaler and was breathing more easily.

Frank was nowhere in sight. The day's activities might be over. A few participants must have concurred because three of them followed the trail down at a slower pace. However, a few groups headed back into the woods once they determined that Dani was being taken care of. Two men helped her up, an older man with a beaked cap over gray hair and a younger, blond one.

The younger one said, "We'll help you back to your car. Did you come with someone?"

She nodded and pointed at me.

"I can drive her car," I said. "Give me her pack. I'll see that she gets home…or to the ER?" I looked at her.

The older man picked up her things and returned them to her pack.

Dani shook her head. "I'm fine now. A bit dizzy. Good thing I had my backup with me." She frowned. "The other one shouldn't have been out yet."

When we reached her car, I brought her pack close to the door and curled my hand around the handle until it beeped twice. That made things easier. I put our equipment in the back seat and drove to her place.

"Mind if I come in and call my brother?"

She nodded. Her color had improved.

Jack took the address and said he'd be along to get me soon.

"I didn't see Frank in the parking lot. I bet he had to go further to get a signal. You get some rest and don't worry about anything. If you need me to run an errand, just let me know. I'll try calling him, but my guess is someone else in the group has already done that." A beep out front startled me. "Are you sure you're okay if I leave you?"

"I'm fine," she said, sitting down and leaning back.

I picked up my things, closed the door behind me, and went out to Jack's car.

As I got in, he said, "What happened to a day in the woods?"

"Dani had an asthma attack. Severe."

I told him what had happened as we drove home. I got out and grabbed my gear. "Oh, yeah. I want to get Alice and Emily's take on today's fun and games. I can also let them know that Dani's fine if Frank hasn't called everyone by dinner time."

We headed into the bungalow.

I dropped my things inside the door and sprinted for the kitchen as my landline rang.

"You really have to call George and get your cell

back." He cleaned up after me.

"Hello? Dani? Calm down. Do you need a ride to urgent care?"

A déjà vu chill scampered down my back, as I remembered the attack on Samantha at the state park last year.

Jack walked up next to me.

I muted the call. "She hasn't said anything I can understand yet."

I finally heard: *Asthma inhaler out of juice.* But I already knew that. I unmuted. "Are you all right?"

Her sharp intake of breath focused my attention. "Frank's dead."

"What are you saying?"

Jack leaned in to try to hear.

"Hang on. There's a speaker button somewhere on this thing."

Jack laughed. "It's not like you didn't use this before you got a cell phone." He punched the button, and Dani's shaky voice filled the room.

Gillian came out of the back bedroom, stretching. "Nap."

I held my index finger to my lips.

She mouthed *Sorry.*

Dani said, "You know this part." She recapitulated. "I had an extra inhaler with me although I can't believe that one was out. I'd barely used it. No cell service. Frank ran off to get help. I pulled my backup out. Who wouldn't take a backup with a life-threatening health issue?"

"Well, thank goodness!"

"Yes, but we left."

"What happened to Frank?"

"He fell off a cliff!"

"What?"

"He fell off a cliff. They couldn't find him."

"Who's *they*?"

"The other members of the group who'd decided to stay behind and enjoy the park and the police."

"How did the police get there if there was no cell service?"

"I don't know. We weren't there, remember?"

"How did you find out about Frank's death and so quickly?"

"They came knocking at my door. They just left." She wheezed.

"Take a breath. Do you have your inhaler?"

"No, they took both."

I looked at Jack, alarmed.

"Hold on," she said.

Then she was back, and I listened to ripping and heavy breathing.

When she spoke, her voice was calm. "The drugstore delivered a new inhaler. Back to normal. I haven't had an attack like this for a while. Sorry."

"No, I'm sorry that I didn't stay with you to make sure you'd be all right. Why did the police take your inhalers?"

"They think someone was trying to kill me. They want to examine them."

"Wait a minute. Why did they think someone was trying to kill you? How did Frank fall? Do they think it was an accident?" I guessed not.

"They found him at the bottom of the cliff on the rocks, at that point where it hangs over the little pool. The water was low. Drought."

"Who found him?"

"I assume it was the police. Some detective named Ho and a woman came to my door. I didn't question them. They didn't like interruptions. I listened and gave them what they wanted."

My heart jumped in my chest. I remembered the handouts. "Jack, get my backpack."

He snatched it up and handed it to me.

I searched through it for the sheets of paper, laying them on the table and smoothing them with my hands. "I'm looking at the handouts Frank gave us when we arrived at the park. He had some team-building things, although I still don't know why he thought that was appropriate, given that you all were vying with each other for a vast inheritance."

Jack picked up one sheet.

I tapped it. "Here. This is a list of all the potential inheritors. If there was an attempt on Dani's life and if Frank was murdered, these are the main suspects. Anyone else involved would have had to have been creeping through the woods, following us, or some random psycho."

"Highly unlikely that they wouldn't have been spotted," Dani said. "The woods weren't dense."

"All these people were with you in the park?" Jack asked.

"With two exceptions." I pointed to a name. "I think this woman, Marilyn Kreski, is dead. I'll explain it to you later, but I saw something about her death."

Jack pointed to my laptop.

I nodded. "Dani, you said two were missing?" I tapped another name. "And this woman, Eliza Renfrew, never showed up, if I counted correctly. I asked people's names as I took pictures. I was taking notes so that I could enter the correct names with their pictures on the portal. Everyone else was on the hike with us, right?"

"Yes," Dani said. "You're right. I didn't see either of them. I didn't meet either in person, but Gen," she paused a moment, "Gen held some video meetings early. We all had our cameras on although some had better resolution than others. Both women were older."

"That's our list of suspects." I touched the sheet with my index finger.

Jack tapped his watch.

I grimaced. "Dani…"

She anticipated me. "Do you really think Alice and Emily will come to dinner at your place tonight?"

"I have no idea."

Jack raised an eyebrow at me.

Gillian said softly, "Coffee?"

I nodded. "Let me think a moment."

Gillian set a mug on the counter next to me.

"Why don't you come along to dinner here tonight, Dani? You probably don't feel like fixing your own dinner, anyway, and you really should eat after such a shock. We have plenty. Also, four people who were on the hike will be here, and we all might be able to get a clear picture of what actually happened."

Chapter 13

At six, Jack let Phil, Alice, and Emily in and took their coats.

Tension filled my dining room, which had always seemed good sized to me…until tonight.

I cleared my throat. "Are you finding the B&B adequate to your needs?"

Phil took a glass from the tray Gillian offered him. "It was up the road a couple of miles as you said. Lovely woman runs it. Nice rooms. Bit pricey."

"This is the California coast in the incipient spring." I raised an eyebrow. "You're probably getting a season price, although maybe not here. Is she full?"

He took a sip. "I was lucky to get a room at the Moon Coast Inn."

"Lots of guests then?" Jack sat opposite Phil.

Alice declined, but Emily took a drink.

They seemed very subdued to me, and I wondered how to broach Frank's death. I wanted to know what they'd seen, but not be too disrespectful.

"Last night we were chatting in Natalie's parlor, and they," Phil nodded toward Alice and Emily, "were telling me that they're here for DNA testing and interviews with Frank Wright from Genevieve Genealogy. Something about inheriting an estate that's worth millions."

"Not Tina Dewey?"

Phil shook his head. "No, he's the one in charge."

I bit my tongue and let him talk.

Gillian set a plate of bruschetta on the coffee table along with a stack of small plates and cocktail napkins.

"It's his company now, and soon the estate may be his. In demonstrating to the relatives how the process would go, he ran his own DNA. Turns out he's a relative, too, possibly her son."

Neither Tina nor Frank had mentioned any of this to me, but I had seen Frank's name on the list. That meant that they all knew and that he hadn't recused himself.

"Unlikely that he's her son. She, as the mother, would know she'd had a child and would have left the estate to him. A father might not know he had a child, but a mother could hardly miss the event. Did you get an idea of how many DNA relatives have turned up?"

"With the eight people staying at the Inn, I'd say there are at least a dozen claimants in town. Who knows how many others will turn up? I told Natalie that I'm not sure how long I'd be staying here. Don't want to lose my room."

I had the impression he was setting the scene to inveigle his way into my home if that happened. My first thought was to ask Jack and Gillian to stay longer to keep my guest room occupied. Then I did a mental head slap. I'm an adult. I can say no.

A rap sounded gently on my door.

"Excuse me." I got up and opened the door to find Dani Boyd, shivering in the chilly air and clutching a bottle of wine. "You'd better come in."

Jack offered her his chair. "Good evening, Professor."

Dani's voice shook from the cold. "We're not on campus. Call me Dani."

He gestured toward the chair. "Have a seat. I can get you something warm to drink, if you'd like. Tea, Irish coffee?"

"Irish coffee sounds delightful. Thanks." She sat next to Gillian, who handed her a shawl from the back of the sofa.

I pointed to it. "My aunt knitted that. It's quite warm."

Dani wrapped it around her shoulders. "I do some knitting myself. I keep meaning to go by that little yarn shop on Oak."

"I was in there yesterday to stroke a few skeins of alpaca. Occasionally, I try knitting something, but it never turns out well."

Gillian responded like one of Pavlov's dogs when the timer went off in the kitchen. "Back in a minute with my latest experiment."

Jack handed Dani her coffee as Gillian reentered with a platter of mushroom puffs.

"Try one of these and let me know what you think. I've been tweaking a few recipes." She handed the platter to Phil. "Pass them around. Phil, this is Dani Boyd, an English professor at Clouston College."

He took a puff and passed them to Alice. "That's a nice little school."

Dani raised an eyebrow. "I like it."

"Phil's my ex-husband," I said.

"Ah."

"Alice, Emily, I assume you know Dani at least from the activity today."

"Yes," Alice said. "We were so worried when you

collapsed. Are you all right?"

Dani smiled. "I am. Thanks. I'm so sorry that I broke up the party."

"I rather think that Frank's death was a more thorough finale," Emily said.

"Of course." Dani glanced down at her hands.

"These are a bit salty," Phil said.

Dani responded as if relieved by the change in topic and bit into one. "Delicious!"

"I concur," Alice said, finishing her puff. "I don't know which was more shocking, your collapse, Dani, or the police rounding us up for questioning. What do you think, Emily?"

"Death is always worse than anything else." Emily selected a puff. "After Frank died and the police intimated that he might have been murdered, we became more worried about you."

"Thank you. I'm much better now. These lovely people kindly invited me to dinner rather than leaving me alone to fend for myself. That's so shocking about Frank. What makes the police think it was murder? He went off by himself."

I cocked my head. "That seems pretty farfetched to me." I didn't want to say too much. I was far more interested in what they thought.

Alice took another puff. "He was on the wrong trail. Not the one that led to the parking lot. There were footprints from a number of different people."

Forensics had been there. I looked at Jack.

Jack said, "Phil was telling us about all the people staying at Moon Coast Inn who are claimants for the Richmond estate. I understand you've all taken DNA tests as part of qualifying as potential heirs. Any surprises?"

Dani said, "I had no idea I was related to the Richmond family until Frank tracked me down and asked me to take the test."

Phil snapped his fingers. "Hey! That's where I saw you. You were talking to Frank."

She raised an eyebrow. "He's been a great source of information about local stories and legends. The Richmond estate inheritance has become a bit of a local legend."

"Why do you care about local legends?" Phil waved his empty cider bottle in the air. "Superstitions."

Jack got up to get him another.

"I must have neglected to mention that, among other classes, I'm covering Folklore this year. I collect stories wherever I go, and I introduce students to their local lore. They're considerably more interested when they can make a personal connection to the stories and legends."

He shrugged absently and accepted the bottle from Jack. His eyes were unfocused, but I couldn't tell if he'd lost the thread of the conversation, or if he didn't care.

Phil took a swig. "I wonder who did the old lady in?"

"What makes you think she was murdered?" Emily had remained quiet, but now she leaned forward.

"Something Frank said about murderers not being able to profit from their crimes."

Now he had my attention. I didn't look directly at him. Instead, I passed the puffs again.

Dani set the shawl aside.

"Dani, would you like something else, now that

you've warmed up?"

She leaned forward to take a puff. "I'll wait for wine with dinner. You mentioned cider. Is that from the haunted distillery?"

"It is. Have you tried it?"

"I'll get her one, Cass." Gillian headed for the kitchen.

"Bring a glass, Gillian," she called over her shoulder. "I'll split it with you."

"According to Frank," Phil said. "The old house on the estate is haunted. Do you believe in ghosts, Cass?"

I had to meet his eyes. "Why, yes, as a matter of fact, I do."

Jack suppressed laughter.

Gillian smiled.

Phil frowned. "Did I miss something?"

I recovered first. "One of the jobs we recently took on has to do with designing an adjunct website for the distillery. They're participating in this year's Coastal Ghost Hop. It's a local ghost tour of our most haunted places."

Gillian carried the now-empty platter out to the kitchen.

"As far as I know, the Richmond estate isn't listed."

"Probably because it's not open to the public," Jack said.

"That'll change," Phil said.

"Oh?"

"Yeah, Frank thinks… thought a lot of people would be interested in a tour of the place. It's expensive to maintain a large house like that, but it could pay for itself."

"Sounds as though he thought he might inherit." That's a motive for murder.

Phil shrugged. "You never know. In any case, Frank took all the legitimate claimants to the inheritance on a hike and a picnic in the state park as sort of a break from all the testing and a chance for them all to get to know each other. Sounds as though he achieved his purpose although not quite in the way he expected. Too bad. He was a good guy."

"It occurs to me that both of the people Tina worked with are now dead," I said.

Chapter 14

"Are you saying you think that lovely girl is a murderer?" Emily said.

I shook my head "She wasn't on the hike, and I know for a fact that she felt as though someone was following her."

"Dani, the young man who helped you has checked out and left town even though the police said to stay here. Steve," Alice said.

"Steve Simons," Dani said.

"He seemed very nervous," Emily added. "We got to the parking lot as you drove away. He said that he's been offered a promotion in Seattle and it wasn't worth his time to stick around to be picked off one by one."

Gillian stood. "Is anyone hungry?"

****

Friday morning dawned crisp and bright, boding well for our Irish party. The house was cleaned, and the decorations hung. Furniture had been rearranged, and fresh flowers cut and placed around the living and dining rooms. Even Thor had been brushed thoroughly and had vanished to sulk in a faraway corner. It would be a quiet and restful day.

As I cut through the resistant green skin of a honeydew melon, I couldn't stop thinking about why Genevieve had been murdered. On the surface, it didn't seem to affect who might inherit or become the caretaker of the estate and the cat. Was I pushing the borders of possibility to think there was something on that flash drive that might point to her murderer?

I opened my laptop and spent a half hour in a fruitless search through all the files I'd uploaded before Jack and Gillian joined me for breakfast, Jack yawning as usual.

Gillian, fresh from her shower and toweling dry her short, ash-blonde hair, asked, "Any luck finding the flash drive?"

I shook my head.

"We'll help look for it after we eat, Cass. Scrambled eggs all round?"

"I'll get the coffee," Jack said. "Cass, do you remember where you last saw it?"

"Yeah, plugged into the side of your laptop."

Jack raised an eyebrow. "Oops." He ran a hand over the edge of his computer. "Not here."

"You carried it back to the bedroom. Can you have a look after you eat to see if it's fallen out onto the floor?"

"Sure thing."

My landline rang. Not having my cell phone was an ongoing pain. I wondered if George was through with it yet.

"Tina, hello… What? Where are you? I'll be right there." I hung up. "Tina says she was attacked. She's at her office. She wants some company. Am I being paranoid for thinking it's a trap?"

"Still have my pocket knife?"

I pulled it out of my jeans pocket and bounced it on the palm of my hand. "Yep. Better than a roll of quarters."

"Don't be silly." Gillian removed the knife from my hand and stuffed it back in her husband's pocket.

"Oooh, do it again."

"Don't be a goof, Jack. Cass, we're going with you."

"But dinner?" I protested.

"Forget dinner," Jack said. "What about breakfast?"

"Cass, you're so not sticking us with cooking dinner while you solve the murder. Jack, we'll send you to the bakery next door to Tina's office. Grab your coats. I'm driving." She pulled on her fleece.

"Has she always been like this?"

"That's why I married her."

The parking lot across the street was half-empty, and I suspected people were taking the day off to celebrate early. As we got out of the car, Jack slipped me the knife and winked at me.

The door was locked. Jack knocked and then peeled off toward the bakery.

A few minutes later, Tina opened the door. When she saw us, she smiled. "I'm glad you're all here, but is Jack coming back? I'd like to lock the door. This place can be really creepy."

"He'll knock again. He's going to the bakery for some coffee and pastries for us," I said.

She locked the door behind us. "I realized that I could look over the files I gave you to try to find out what infuriated Frank so much." She led us into her office. "I think he was murdered."

"So do I." I sat across from her at the desk. "Too much of a coincidence, otherwise."

Gillian pulled up chairs for Jack and herself.

"Are you all right? Who attacked you? Did you see a doctor?" I asked.

"I don't know. They were searching my apartment. Hit me from behind. Knocked me out. Saw my GP. I do have a concussion, but I couldn't go back home. I keep a change of clothes here. There's a security system and cameras, so I'm camping out." She opened a drawer and pulled out a carving knife.

Jack rapped heavily at the door, making us all jump.

"You're right. The office is atmospheric when mostly empty." I stood. "That'll be Jack. I do feel that I need that coffee he's bringing."

"I'll let him in." Tina scooted around the desk and headed for the front door.

"She's still carrying the knife," Gillian said.

We followed her down the hall, but she got there first and opened it.

"Whoa!" Jack leaned back. "It's just me."

"Oh, I'm so sorry. Didn't realize." Tina dropped her arm to her side. "Come in."

"You realize you have to get close to use that effectively." Jack kept his gaze on the knife as he moved around her.

"I don't have a gun or taser. Or a baseball bat, for that matter. I cook and do genealogy. That's it." She led us back down the hall to her office and placed the knife back in the drawer.

"Boyfriend?" Gillian asked.

She hesitated but shook her head.

I wasn't convinced. Her glance didn't meet mine but darted all around the room as she denied it. Somewhere, there was a boyfriend.

"Girlfriend?" Gillian asked.

She shook her head again, this time decisively. "Pathetic, isn't it?"

"No," I said. "At the moment, my stats are the same." That was more or less true… at the moment.

"Much as your love life is fascinating," Jack said, "Tina, you must have called us for a reason other than bodyguard services. What did you find?"

"Oh, yeah." She turned her computer monitor around so that we could see it. "Gen found a lot of potential inheritors, but when she started to contact them, she found out that quite a few of them were dead."

"What's unusual about that?"

"They died recently. Many were young. Some did die of apparent illnesses, and some were quite elderly. There were a bunch of accidents, which could be murders. Gen did the statistics, and the number of people in the sample who had fatal accidents was way beyond chance."

I leaned back in the chair. "She thought someone was killing off the competition."

Tina nodded. "All over the United States and England."

"Wow." England. "Travel should be traceable." Was George aware of this? Two reasons to contact him now. My pulse quickened. But I tamped the feeling down quickly. After Doris' stunt, he'd be in no mood to talk to me. "More deaths in the US or England?"

"If you're wondering whether the killer is English or American, there are no longer any relatives in England," Tina said. "An entire branch of the family wiped out. A small branch, but nonetheless…" She started to cry. "I'm sorry. Sometimes it's too much."

I wanted to ask more, but I couldn't push her now. She seemed so fragile.

"You haven't had time to grieve."

She grabbed a tissue. "It's been good to have something to do."

Gillian leaned forward. "But the attack on you happened after Frank died, yet Frank was the one who was upset that Cass might see this information. Sounds like the attacker was looking for this data, also. Who else knew about it?"

"All of the potential candidates who are here locally for the final selection, including your friend, the professor." Tina blew her nose and threw the tissue away.

"Maybe the person who hit you also pushed Frank off the cliff." Jack and I exchanged a look.

She pursed her lips. "That would mean that it was someone in the group that went to the state park."

Jack shook his head. "Not necessarily. Anyone who knew about the expedition could have followed them and shoved Frank when he was alone. Or it could have been a psycho. Or it could have been an accident. Although I agree that an inheritor is the most likely."

"Can you print this out for me?" I tapped her monitor.

"Don't you have it already? I'm sure I put all the files on the drive."

"My sister seems to have misplaced the drive." Jack smirked at me.

I really hated it when he talked about me in the third person as if I weren't there.

Tina sat up straighter. "Or whoever hit me was in

your home, knew about the drive, saw it, and stole it."

Chills coursed up my spine. "Only one person who was at the state park has been in my house."

Jack, Gillian, and I exchanged a knowing glance. "Dani."

"The professor?" Tina hit *print*, and the printer down the hall started grinding. "Why was she at your house?"

"She was there for dinner. And she's coming back tonight for the party."

Tina grimaced. "Do you mind if I change my RSVP to a no?"

Chapter 15

"No." I laughed. "But my ex will be there, so I'll be more worried than you."

"That'll be awkward."

"Yep. I so want him to be guilty, but he has no motive. In fact, motive has been what we've been short of in trying to figure Gen's murder out. Frank's murder could be gain although he's not listed in the competition. With the others you mentioned, I think the clear motive for their murders is gain. How many were killed? I do think you should call Sebastian Kane and tell him about what happened to you."

Gillian added, "You might also want to follow up with your doctor."

I rose. "I'll grab the printout. I think we should swing by Dani's place on our way home to have a talk with her. But we do have to go to finish up the dinner prep. I hope to see you there later."

I thumbed through the pages as I returned to her office.

Tina got up. "I guess I'll be safe at your house. I'll walk you to the door."

"See you then."

Back at the car, Gillian said, "Why don't you drop us off, and we'll work on dinner. I think you'll be fine talking to Dani alone. I don't get a killer vibe from her. She might have stolen the flash drive for information, though."

I started the car and headed for home. "Hope you're right."

Dani's address was on the printout I'd gotten from Tina, but I pulled over a block down to check that I'd remembered it correctly. I looked up in time to see her open the back of a gray SUV. Then she dragged a heavy, green canvas bag about six feet long to the back of the SUV, and struggled as she lifted it inside.

My suspicious mind screamed: "Body!" But could she lift a body? She was definitely on the young side and athletic. Probably about five–foot, ten inches. I fought an inner struggle. Should I confront her or call the cops? George wasn't exactly thrilled with me these days, and he'd most likely take the call. Even if Bill or Rusty responded, all three of them were as tight as… The cliché came to mind, but the three were closer than peas in a pod could ever be.

No, it had to be me. Jack used the friend locator function on his phone to find me all the time. If she didn't ditch my phone, they could at least find my body. And then I remembered. George still had my phone. I hesitated. But then I swallowed, turned the car around, and circled back to pull up right behind her car.

Dani stopped trying to lift the body into the back, pushed a lock of hair behind her ear, and stared at me as I got out and approached her.

She blinked as she laughed. "Your timing is perfect. Can you help me with this?" She indicated the body bag.

I swallowed to keep from throwing up. "Sure thing." I wondered if I'd have time to unzip it to see who the victim was.

She climbed into the back. "If you can shove it even a little, I think I can pull it in here."

Before I touched the bag, I looked for leaking blood and hoped the victim didn't have a communicable disease.

"Don't let any of the needles prick you," Dani said.

I dropped my end and jumped back.

Dani held onto her side of the bag, but frowned at me. "What's the matter? Afraid of a few pricks?"

"What kind of needles are in there?"

Dani set the bag down carefully, tilted her head, and squinted as if she were seeing me for the first time. "Fir, of course, or whatever composite they're using to fake it these days."

I frowned at her. "What are you talking about?"

"My artificial Christmas tree. What did you…?" And then she laughed until she snorted, collapsing over the bag.

I stood there totally confused.

"Oh, my gosh!" she said, gasping. "You thought I'd asked you to help me…" Another scream of laughter. When that subsided, she said, "Cass, you really are a good friend if you were willing to help me move a body!"

Still giggling, she climbed over to the zipper and unzipped the bag, revealing a pre-lit, artificial Christmas tree. "See? Not a murderer."

I exhaled. "Glad we got that cleared up." Then I started to laugh, too.

Dani began again and wiped her eyes. Our conversation for a few minutes consisted only of words, phrases, and wild gestures until we calmed down. Together, we got the tree into her car.

"C'mon inside for some coffee before I ask if you'll come with and help me get this monster into a storage unit."

"Of course. What are friends for?"

That started us laughing again.

I wiped away my tears. "You're coming to my dinner tonight, right?"

"Wouldn't miss it. Is this like one of those movies where they gather all the suspects together and reveal how it was done?" Dani closed and locked her SUV.

"I hope not. My brother would be really pissed to think I suspected him of murder! Besides, I have no idea how either murder was committed. You didn't shove Frank off the cliff, did you?"

I followed her into her house, which was far more modern than mine. As she was a visiting professor, I assumed this was a rental.

"No, but his mother might have." She led the way into the kitchen, where she made coffee and set out sugar and cream.

"His mother?" I paused in the act of lifting the lid off the sugar.

She set out a plate of homemade chocolate chip cookies. "I overheard them arguing. Only husbands and wives or mothers and their children argue like that. No holds barred. He called her 'a senile old bat.' Moments later, he was dead."

"I would have considered shoving someone off a cliff for calling me that." I thought back to the list. "There was no Mrs. Wright on that hike."

"No, but there was a Mrs. Wainwright. Sue Wainwright."

I did remember that name. "He changed his name."

Dani sat and fixed her coffee, not stinting on the cream. "And he didn't put himself down as a possible inheritor-slash-caretaker, either."

"Do the police know?"

She shrugged. "I didn't tell them. I didn't care for their interrogation techniques. I'm afraid I was a bit uncooperative." She paused and smiled. "Although there was one rather attractive detective."

"George Ho."

"That's him. You know him? Of course. You're a local."

I swallowed.

Her eyes narrowed. "No, it's more than that. I don't mean to pry, but—"

I held up a hand. "Not now. I can't get into it today with so much I still have to do. I'll tell you later." I finished my coffee and cookie. "I've got to get going. See you tonight."

As I drove off, it occurred to me that she *was* strong enough to move a body.

Chapter 16

When I got back home, I tossed my bag on the couch and headed to the kitchen for a cup of coffee. I leaned on the counter to look at my check-off list for the party.

"I'm bored." Doris materialized on the kitchen counter in her tap-dancing shorts, slender legs crossed.

I stifled a small scream.

"Seriously? You should be used to me by now."

I ignored her jibe. "How can you be bored? You're a ghost. Don't you have access to the ethereal realms or something?" I poured the cup of coffee in an attempt to jumpstart my own enthusiasm for tonight's get-together.

She uncrossed her legs and leaned forward, elbows on knees. "Would I be hanging out here if I did?"

"I thought you liked spending time with me." I took a sip.

She snorted.

I raised an eyebrow. "I guess I know where *I* stand. How long have you been haunting this house?"

"More than a half-dozen decades, I think. Why?"

"Are you often bored?"

She leaned so close that her ethereal presence cooled me. "Not since you arrived." She swanned back and raised the back of her hand to her brow. "Until now."

"Perhaps you should take this quiet time to chill?"

She sat bolt upright. "Chill? How much more chill can I get than dead?"

She had a point.

Jack came in. "Enough coffee for me?"

I gestured toward the pot.

Jack poured a cup. "By the way, I saw Thor eating a spider. Are you feeding him enough?"

"No, I thought I'd starve him so that he'll eat more spiders."

"Are you—" Then he caught on. "I believed you there for a moment."

I opened my laptop as I heard a knock at the door.

Jack answered it, and I heard him say, "Dani—"

I shut my laptop and got up to talk to her.

Her phone pinged. She held it up to show me. "There's a tracking device moving with me."

"Your phone told you that?"

"The manufacturer of my cell phone makes the tracking device that is being used to track me, so, yes, my phone told me so." She held the phone up so that I could see the map and the icon that was with her. "This is the first time it pinged, so I'm guessing your murder suspect list is also the suspect list for whoever planted this on me."

"Including Frank," I said.

Her eyes widened. "You're right. That's spooky. Tracked from beyond the grave."

I wondered if the police had his phone, had hacked in, and could now tell where Dani was.

She stared off into space, and for a moment, I thought Doris had appeared, but she seemed to be thinking.

"Dani…"

She refocused on me.

"You realize that everyone on the hike is a suspect in trying to kill you, but you are also a suspect in Frank's murder?"

She shook her head. "No, for the attempt on me, it could have been done much earlier if someone deliberately emptied my inhaler as opposed to my not recalling correctly how many times I used it previously. The only way it could have actually been done on the hike is if an empty canister was shoved into my inhaler. It would have had to have been preplanned. Frank's fall could have been an accident or a spur of the moment impulsive murder." Her head jerked back. "Oh, I see. You think I might have pushed him. But why? Not to mention that I was with you being helped down the mountain when he ran off never to be seen alive again."

"Not really because I'm your alibi, but we have to put you on the suspect list because the police will. We'll have to figure out what they know." I looked down at Thor. "And I think I know a way to do that." Should I tell her about Doris?

She frowned. "I may have smudged any fingerprints on the canister when I was trying to figure out what was wrong with it."

"My guess is that the killer would have wiped it or worn gloves if your murder was preplanned. I thought the point of the heirs list was that the next inheritor in each branch of the family was part of this gathering. That would mean…"

Dani nodded. "Yes. Frank's mother would inherit. Frank was there as the facilitator. If you were trying to knock off your competition, she would have been the target, not Frank. That explains why he wasn't on the list."

"It seemed odd to me until you told me about his mother. I'm sure Tina and Gen knew, also."

"Can we assume that?" Dani asked.

"No, but if they did, that eliminates the motive for his murder, to advance a candidate to a better position to inherit. Maybe killing him was more personal than that. He wasn't very nice."

"Or a mistake. I haven't heard people talking against him, and your ex seems to like him."

"Unlikely to be a mistake. Accident, yes; mistake, no. You probably noticed that most of the inheritors are women."

"True. And your point?"

I shook my head. "Just noodling." Then I remembered what Phil had said. "You met my ex last night. He said Frank thought he might have been the woman's son. I said she would have known if she had a child to whom to leave her estate. But maybe he misheard a conversation that was about Frank and his mother?"

"Hmm. Possible."

"Dani, do you consider yourself open-minded?"

She cocked her head. "Where are you going with this?"

"You're a folklore professor."

"True."

"You study unusual things."

She crossed her arms over her chest. "And your point?"

"You said you don't believe in ghosts."

"I haven't seen one."

"Would you like to?"

She raised an eyebrow. "I don't want to go on a local ghost walk in drizzly rain and capture raindrops on my lens only to be told they're ghost orbs."

"If that's what you thought I was proposing, you're going to love this." I looked up at the ceiling. Lately, she'd been descending from my loft above our heads. "Doris!"

Dani followed my gaze and also looked up, so we both missed Doris' entrance until she ran a hand through Dani's shoulder, inducing the most blood-curdling scream I'd ever heard.

Adrenaline flushed cold through my veins. "Doris!"

"You rang?"

Doris was dressed in green. My first thought was Robin Hood, before I realized.

"A leprechaun? Really?"

"Tis the season. What do you think?" She twirled around in front of us, held her hands up, and changed her nail polish to green in the blink of an eye. Then she whirled around and stared at Dani.

I realized that Dani had poked Doris in the back.

Doris went all hands-on-hips. "Checking to see if I'm a hologram?" She turned to me. "Why do your friends always think I'm technology?"

I shrugged. "It's the modern age, and folks are a bit more skeptical than they were when you died in the Twenties."

Dani walked around her, looking up and down. "Disappear."

Doris vanished.

"Reappear."

Doris returned.

"Can you change your size?"

Doris shrank to the size of a mouse. Dani laughed delightedly. Doris had never been this cooperative with me nor had I ever known her to follow orders with alacrity.

"Forgive me," I said. "Your reaction to my resident ghost is a bit, shall we say, unusual?" I hadn't meant it as a question, but my voice squeaked at the end of the sentence.

"I've seen some strange stuff in my explorations and research. I've seen people's aspect change in dark ceremonies. I've watched objects seem to defy the laws of physics as we know them. And then there's quantum mechanics or, as Einstein called it, spooky interaction at a distance. But this is different. She's different."

Doris regarded Dani as intensely as Dani gazed at her.

Dani indicated Doris with a wave of her hand. "Can't we send... Doris ... into the police station to find out what they know?"

I cleared my throat. "Dani, this is Doris. Doris, this is Dani. Dani, Doris has some limitations. She can't leave the premises without a ride, a physical entity to carry her ectoplasmic self over the boundary, whatever it is."

"You're talking about possession." She shivered. "I've seen that, too. And zombies."

"Werewolves?"

"They don't exist."

"You can say that after meeting Doris?"

She shrugged. "I haven't run into any... yet."

"Good to know." And I meant it.

127

"Back to Doris. Does she possess you?"

"Don't give her ideas."

"I'm right here. I use Thor, Cass' cat, as my transport most of the time. Before Cass moved in, I occasionally used a passing squirrel or mouse. Bats give me a headache."

"Ghosts can get headaches? Isn't that a physical thing?"

"Metaphorical headache. All that squeaking. Mice are almost as bad."

Dani laughed. "The practical side of ghosting." She pulled out her phone and dictated a note about a lecture on ghosts. Tucking her phone in her pocket, she said, "It's a great idea for a lecture. Should up the attendance."

"I'm sure Doris would be delighted to provide you with more practical details, but maybe you could help us out first, Doris? Want to pay another visit to the police department?"

There was a knock at the door.

Doris vanished and reappeared. "Not necessary. The police have come to you." She disappeared again.

The second knock was harsher.

I opened the door. "Hi, George. C'mon in." I stepped aside.

George walked in. "Professor Boyd, I presume?"

"That would be me."

"We'll need your fingerprints for elimination and a statement as you weren't on the scene when we arrived. You can come with me to the station to take care of both now."

The shock I felt was mirrored on Dani's face. George hadn't issued an invitation to help the police.

The tone of his voice was definitely accusatory. Did he consider Dani a suspect?

"How's the investigation going?"

He was cool and distant as he frowned at me. "You know better than to ask that."

"No harm in trying." I tried to say it in a brisk and uncaring fashion, adding a smile to my face for good measure. I was rewarded with a tiny upturn in the corner of his mouth and a quick glimpse at the George of old. I raised a hand to the small ache in my chest. "Also, I was with Dani from the inhaler incident all the way back to her house. I drove her, in fact."

He nodded and made a note. "Thank you. Have you already given a statement to that effect?"

"You know I haven't."

"Then please come down to the station yourself to make a statement." He closed his little notebook.

"Is this a good time to ask about my cell phone?"

Dani grabbed her bag. "I'll see you later, Cass." She followed George out.

I closed the door behind them and started to call out, but Doris anticipated me and shimmered two feet above the floor, bobbing like an apple at Halloween.

"Feel like an adventure?"

"Always!"

Chapter 17

While Thoris was down at the police station, I got back to work, transferring the information from Frank's handouts to our spreadsheet. The headers were the usual: Suspects, Means, Motive, Opportunity, and Comments. Under suspects, I listed all the DNA relatives: Alice Wembley, Dani Boyd, Sue Wainwright, Julio Fuentes, Emily Beaton, Steve Simmons, Marilyn Kreski, and Eliza Renfrew. Eight relatives all had different last names from a couple different ethnicities.

I was a bit surprised, but I guess it was a span of over a hundred years with quite a few marriages and no direct-line descendants. That would have been too easy. There must have been more. Descendants mushroomed over the years. Some must have decided not to respond, and some probably thought it was a scam. Frank could have been disqualified or not been interested. Not that it mattered now.

I stopped and leaned back in the chair. Motive. Gaining control over the fortune and a very nice house to live in.

The banging on my front door was worthy of the Norse gods howling

As I turned toward the racket, Doris rolled like a cannon ball through the middle of the door and vanished into the ether. I hesitated, but opened the door.

George stood on my doorstep like an angry tiki god. In one clenched fist he held a wire animal cage that contained a very disgruntled Thor. He thrust it at me. "Here. Didn't you think I'd recognize your cat and know why he was there? Don't try any more of these shenanigans. Your spies are not welcome at the station."

I took the cage from him, receiving a light shock as our fingers brushed for a moment. "Shenanigans?"

Without a word, he stomped down my steps to his car and peeled out of my yard.

I thought we'd made progress lately. If we had, that tiny edge of gain was gone now. I closed the door, set the cage down, and released Thor, who growled and headed for his food dish in the kitchen.

"Doris!"

Nothing.

I whispered, "Doris."

Doris faded in slowly as I'd never seen her before. Instead of her usual flapper attire and bobbed dark hair, she wore her hair in loose curls. Her knee-length dress flowed softly around her, white flowers on navy blue. The change frightened me. She seemed younger.

"Are you all right?"

"That was terrifying."

"What does it take to scare a ghost?"

"A very angry cop." She performed an exaggerated, full-body shiver. "I hate to say this, but cute as he is, I no longer think you should pursue him. He's scary."

I tried very hard to suppress my rueful laugh. "I don't think there's any danger of that any more. I think we're over. Were you able to find out anything before he captured you?"

"Not much. I'll have to go back." She glanced at Thor as he sauntered out of the kitchen, licking his chops. "But not with my usual ride. I'll have to find a squirrel or something."

"But what did you find out?"

She faded halfway. "Something that might break this case wide open." Then she vanished.

My turn to growl. "Doris!"

So frustrating, but given that I was stuck for a more granular motive and still had work to do on the ghost hop, I didn't think about what she was getting up to until I received a phone call from Detective Rusty Riordan, my least favorite of George's fellow officers.

"Thought you might like to know that shortly after your cat paid us a visit at the station, an athletic little chipmunk also showed an uncommon interest in our case notes pertaining to the murder of Frank Wright," she said.

"He was murdered?" I heard her suck her teeth.

"We treat all deaths as suspicious until we're sure."

Something about her tone of voice made me hyperaware. What did she know? Had George told her about Doris? Was she making a connection between the cat and the chipmunk or was I being paranoid?

"It is interesting that the autopsies of Frank and the chipmunk will both take place this afternoon."

I gasped.

"I had a feeling you'd be interested." She disconnected.

She knew! "Rusty! Wait!"

Too late. I had to know what she was alluding to for sure, and I had to rescue Doris. Never mind that she was dead, she was my roommate and friend. I didn't want her to vanish permanently.

That was pretty selfish. Amend to, "I didn't want her to vanish permanently unless it was to go into the light." Yes. However, it was also pretty irritating that she hadn't told me what she saw that would break the case wide open. Typical Doris. I ground my teeth and banged both fists on the counter. I needed a plan.

An autopsy meant the chipmunk would be dead by this afternoon and maybe my ghost along with the critter. She wouldn't be able to get home to safety before her host was destroyed. George had brought her back inside the boundary when he carried Thor home. I had to think.

Mia and Ricardo were in class. George knew all of my friends and would be suspicious if any of them walked into the station. Who could I call who wouldn't think I was stark-staring mad? Mina.

She answered on the second ring. "Hello?"

"We have to get you a cell phone."

Her laugh was a high-pitched peal. "Hello, dear."

"I need help."

"We all do from time to time."

"It's a bit sticky. I think Doris is inhabiting a chipmunk, and they caught her in the station. They're planning to autopsy her this afternoon."

Silence. Then two words: "Oh, dear." She hung up.

"Mina?" Had I frightened her off?

Apparently not. She rapped at my door five minutes later.

"Come in."

"Tea?"

"Of course."

I led the way to my kitchen, flicked on the electric kettle, and turned to her. "I have no idea how to rescue the chipmunk and Doris."

"Why are they autopsying a chipmunk?"

"Oolong?"

"Do you still have some of the white jasmine?"

"I do." I filled my little metal tea ball with loose tea.

"Heat the cup first."

"Of course."

We were silent while the tea steeped.

After Mina's first sip, she said, "Perhaps Prissy could help. Cats do chase chipmunks. George has never seen Prissy."

"Would he be able to see her now?"

"I think that would be up to Prissy."

"I'm guessing that a ghost can't inhabit a ghost, so Doris wouldn't be able to guide her."

"She's a spirit, Cass. I think once she understands the situation, she'll be able to handle it although she may…" Mina looked off into the distance.

I didn't even pretend to understand what she was talking about. Perhaps I'd called the wrong person for help. But I knew, even as I thought it, that there was no one else who could assist with this kerfuffle. My only other choice would be to walk into the station and tell them they couldn't kill the chipmunk because they'd also be killing my ghost. They'd section me for sure.

Had Rusty manipulated me into this? She didn't like me. Why would she call me and think I'd be interested in a chipmunk autopsy? Did I even know if it was the truth? Why would they want to autopsy a chipmunk? What the heck was going on?

I rubbed the bridge of my nose. "I have such a headache." I was probably being paranoid, but for a moment I wondered if George had told her what to say, just to yank my chain.

Mina patted my other hand. "You need plausible deniability. Where are Jack and Gillian?" She looked around.

I checked my watch. "They're due back soon. Shopping for a couple extra things for dinner tonight. You're coming, aren't you?"

"If I'm able. Now, stick with them until it's all over. You must have witnesses that you were not in the vicinity of the police station."

"Okay. I can do that. What are you going to do?"

She smiled. "I love animals. I'm going to rescue a chipmunk. Behave yourself. Don't get curious. I'll tell you all about it later." She stood. "Trust me."

I opened the door to see Jack and Gillian approaching.

As Mina passed them, she said, "Don't let her out of your sight for the next few hours."

I held the door for them.

Gillian turned and watched her walk off.

"What the heck was that all about?" Jack asked as he carried the supplies into the kitchen.

"What have you been up to now?" Gillian set her bag down on the dining room table and pulled green, shiny decorations out of it.

"Not me. Doris. Mina thinks she knows a way to save Doris from the chipmunk autopsy."

Jack yelled from the kitchen, "I think I need a beer before you tell us *this* story. You guys want anything?"

"Lemonade," Gillian said.

"I think I need a Long Island Iced Tea."

Jack laughed. "You got it."

When we were all seated, I explained Thoris' mission, the capture, and Doris' comment about catching a ride back with a squirrel. "So, when Rusty called and said they'd captured a chipmunk that was trying to read the autopsy report, I assumed that Doris had indeed gone back. Mina thinks she knows a way to save her, but we can't go near the station. You guys have to provide me with an alibi for anything that happens down there."

Jack's eyes widened, but Gillian burst out laughing.

When she stopped, she wiped her tears. "This might be the craziest thing you've done yet."

Jack shook his head. "You were so responsible when you were married to Phil. Midlife crisis much?"

Chapter 18

After lunch, my doorbell rang. Almost no one used it because they couldn't figure out how it worked. Leave it to Mina to know. You had to turn the "key," which was a key head-shaped protrusion to the right side of the door that caused an old bell, like the ones on kids' bicycles in the Fifties, to ring. A little hammer hit a metal shell, creating a ring that sounded more like shaking a box of rocks than a bell.

My heart skipped a beat. I hoped she'd been successful.

Gillian beat me to the door. "I don't think I've ever heard that before." She held the door open.

Mina entered, carrying a small cat carrier that she set on the dining room table. Before she opened the door, she said, "Doris, dear, why don't you walk the chipmunk out onto the porch before you leave her? She has babies to attend to."

Gillian had half-closed the door, but she opened it again. "How do you know that?"

Mina opened the carrier. "She's lactating."

"How do you know *that*?" Jack asked.

Mina smiled.

The chipmunk stepped out, scanned the room, and hopped to the floor, heading for the door. At the threshold, she stopped, sat on her haunches, and waved at us before bounding outside.

Gillian quickly shut the door.

Doris floated in through the door and toward Mina. Mina held up a hand. "No hugs!"

"What happened?" I said to both of them, suppressing a laugh at the expression on Mina's face as she repulsed Doris' cold, wet affection.

Doris did a full-body shiver. "That chipmunk was lactating."

"Doris!"

"All right! All right! Well, Thor and I tried sneaking around low when we entered the station the first time, but you know how big Thor is. We hid under a desk until George went to the bathroom. We weren't fast enough when he got back. I had my eye on him, but Rusty got us by the scruff of the neck."

"But what did you see? You said it was something that would blow the case wide open."

"I might have exaggerated a little bit." She squinted and held up her thumb and index finger with a tiny bit of space between them.

"*Doris.*"

"They found a partial print from Frank on Dani's inhaler. When I went back, the paper was no longer on top. I was shuffling the papers with my tiny paws when they caught me. They had a list of the heirs. Dani's name is on it. They made a connection between one of the heirs and Frank, who was not on the list, but George had written his name at the bottom with a question mark. Frank's autopsy is pending. If the woman is related, she hasn't come forward to claim the body. And that's as far as I got before they nabbed me."

"Mina, how did you get the chipmunk?"

She chuckled. "That was easy. I told George that

you were perplexed by Rusty's phone call. I happened to be at your house, having tea, which was true, and told you that it sounded as though they'd captured my pet chipmunk. I'd train her from a pup. He said to prove it. This was the sticky bit because I didn't know if Doris was really in there, but I gave her voice commands, and Doris performed like a circus veteran. You should have seen her sitting up and playing dead. Everybody trusts little old ladies." Mina pursed her lips. "You need to be careful, Cass. Rusty does not like you, and she's making a play for George. He seems to be buying into what she's saying about you lying and being devious and using him."

Doris went hands on hips. "Told you. If he believes her, he's not worth it. She's the one who yelled rabid when she saw me. She grabbed me with thick gloves, looked into my eyes, and said they were going to euthanize and dissect me. It was as if she knew that would leave me out in the cold with nowhere to go. He must have told her about me. No bugs or animals in a clean room where the autopsy would take place. George came in just as they were getting ready to put me down, so I jumped into him." Her gaze unfocused, as if she were watching something in the distance.

"Are you all right?"

"It was weird. He knew I was there. I felt his emotions. Turmoil. Betrayal. He's aware and furious but he sounds like a madman. I couldn't control him. He's yelling 'Get out. Get out.'" Doris shook herself. "They sent him home to rest and to see a shrink. I was trying to decide between the chipmunk and the doctor when Mina came in and saved the day." She smiled at Mina. "I hopped into the chipmunk in time to follow

Mina's orders. I'm afraid I left George with a bit of a headache." Then she frowned at me. "But, Cass, Tina's name and Frank's were crossed out, and Dani's name was written all over in caps and underlined. Looks like she's his main suspect now that Frank's dead." She paused. "Unless he's off the case." Then her forehead furrowed "That would put Rusty in charge. Ewww." She did a full-body shiver and vanished.

Jack and Gillian had been largely silent. Then they started talking at once.

"Tea?" I said.

Mina smiled. "Yes, please."

"Is Phil coming tonight?" Gillian asked.

"I could hardly not invite him."

"Is that why you never married, Mina? To avoid awkward parties with exes?" Gillian took the last of the coffee and rinsed the pot out.

Mina sipped her tea, looked out the kitchen window, and focused on the past. "What makes you think I never married?"

I tried to remember what had given me that impression. "No mention of a husband, no pictures of one in your house. No missus."

She smiled as she set her delicate bone china cup back in its saucer. "I've had not one but two husbands: a city mouse and a country mouse."

My impressions of Mina changed instantly. "What happened?"

"Prepare yourself. My life isn't what you think." She smiled at all of us.

Even Doris hung around to hear what she had to say.

"I was raised in northern Wisconsin in a town

you've never heard of, in one of the most beautiful parts of this country that most people have never seen. My childhood was spent wandering freely. Remember how old I am. It was a different time. I canoed alone or with my best friend. Portaged my canoe from lake to lake. And it was a canoe. Not a kayak or paddle board. Wood, not plastic. I'm a fair shot with a bow and arrow, and I can tell you where to find wild asparagus and strawberries."

I leaned back, coffee forgotten, staring at her.

She laughed. "But I didn't value the treasure my life held back then. As soon as I could, I headed for the big city to the south where I fell in love with a native city dweller. He knew how to ride the El—the elevated train. He took me to the Loop and the John Hancock building and the Water Tower. It was magic." She stopped smiling. "Until it wasn't."

"I'm so sorry."

"Me, too, but I wasn't ready to go home although my dad said he'd drive down to get me. No, instead I set out for the west where I met a hard-drinking, hard-riding cowboy. You should have seen those arm muscles from all that roping and wrangling!"

I stared at Mina, trying to picture this slender, bird-like older woman, dressed head-to-toe in wispy lavender, lusting after a hunky cowboy.

Mina nodded. "My mother had the same look on her face when I went home for Christmas to tell the family that I was getting married again. That marriage lasted three years: one of bliss, one of rage, one of tears. Beware of passion. It has a dark side. That's why it often leads to murder."

"Is this your way of telling me that you bumped off

your husband?"

Her smile was back. "It's my way of telling you that only psychopaths kill coldly." She tapped the newspaper between us. "They've got it all wrong."

"Is this your way of distracting me from your love life?"

"My dear, my life has been so much calmer since I foreswore men." She looked around at all of us. "And since they both died."

We gasped.

"No, I didn't kill them."

"Of course, you didn't," I said hastily.

With a smile, Mina finished her tea and stood. "Speaking of exes, Cass, I think you'd be missing a bet if you didn't invite that nice police detective you like so much."

Is that what she'd come to tell me? Why?

"Two exes at the same party? Wouldn't that lead to murder?" Jack joked.

The corners of Mina's eyes crinkled. "It would certainly put the cat among the pigeons."

"You're a troublemaker, Mina."

"You've only noticed that now?" She winked at him. "I believe I will withdraw my acceptance to your kind offer for your party and leave my space open for George. I rather think you'll need it."

I started to protest, but she was right about needing the space.

She clucked her tongue. "Quit trying to manage things. Let them play out. Let people get angry. When they do, they reveal the truth. You keep prettying up the place. Let the fur fly. See what happens. Don't you want to know the truth?" Her eyes narrowed. "Or are you afraid of what you might find out?"

Sweet, subtle Mina shocked me. Was she talking about murderers or exes? Was I afraid? If I were being honest with myself, I was avoiding confrontation. I stopped. I always avoided confrontation. I didn't like it. I had a nasty feeling that I was going to be very uncomfortable tonight.

Mina stared at me until I nodded. Then she touched me briefly on the upper arm, so lightly that I almost didn't feel it. "You know what they say about the truth."

Perhaps I needed the freedom she was referring to.

She winked at me and left.

Gillian said, "What was that all about?"

I sighed. "I have to invite George."

"Are you crazy?" Jack asked.

"Probably, but she's right. This will be so awkward on so many levels." I picked up my landline.

I think George was shocked that I invited him, and I was equally stunned that he accepted, particularly after our recent interactions.

"Could you bring my phone? Pretty please?"

"We'll see."

I thought about tranquilizers and gin but didn't do either. Instead, I fussed about everything.

Jack and Gillian stayed out of my way.

Chapter 19

Doris' head materialized while I was up in my loft, trying to decide what to wear. "Is it safe?"

"I could use the company. I can't decide between the green because George would like it or the navy because it's not flattering."

"I get it. You want to attract George, but not Phil. You don't really have a choice. It's St. Patrick's Day. You have to go with the green. You're divorced. Phil has no hold over you."

"You say that, but…" But what? Why did I allow him to influence me? "You're right. It suits the day, and I do want George to find me attractive although heaven only knows why. He certainly hasn't been very nice to me lately."

Doris' laughter echoed across the eaves. "And you've been so lovely to him, sending me to spy on him."

"Doris!"

"Maybe he's trying to protect you."

"From what?"

"Getting killed? You do tend to put yourself in the middle of some rather threatening situations sometimes. Like that hike."

"Not my fault."

"Keep telling yourself that."

"Go check on the others. It's almost time. Please

remember that not everyone at the party has met you. Keep the chaos to a minimum, all right?"

"I'll try, but if people will insist on using electronics, what can I do?"

"Quit sticking your ghostly hand through their phones or their stomachs. I want them to think I'm a good cook!"

Her laughter faded more slowly than she did.

*****

George arrived early. "We need to talk. Put on a jacket and come with me."

I followed him down to the beach. "We can be seen."

"I don't care about being seen. I care about being overheard." He stuffed his hands in his pockets. "You look lovely, by the way."

"Thank you. You do, too."

He smiled and then looked serious. "Please be careful. You've invited a mixed bag tonight. Were you trying to bring all the suspects together?"

"No, I'm not doing a whodunit reveal or anything. These are all people I've been involved with lately…except for you."

"Sorry about that. It's just the cat and the chipmunk…" He looked toward the ocean.

I had to find out. "Does Rusty know about Thoris?"

He shook his head. "No. Rusty knows nothing about ghosts or possession. She thought you'd sent sick animals into the station as revenge on me. She warned me against you and has from the beginning, saying that my relationship with the local 'nut job' threatens my advancement on the force."

"You've been walking a bit of a tightrope at work." Was this where he told me we were through forever? My stomach roiled.

"There are times when you do threaten my credibility." He softened his rebuke with a smile.

I looked down. "Sorry 'bout that."

"No, you're not, but I'm up for a promotion, and we do get peer reviews."

"Point taken, but there are a few things—"

"No."

"But—"

"Not tonight."

"Tomorrow?"

"We'll see."

I tilted my head toward him. He bent slightly. I closed my eyes.

Jack yelled, "Cass!"

The moment evaporated.

George hugged me to him and laughed. "Old times."

Being held by him felt so comfortable. "It's hard to get a break."

He kissed the top of my head. "I'm here tonight for you…if you need me."

I always need you. "Thank you."

We walked back.

Guests were arriving as we reached the porch. Old friends pulled into my yard, which was mostly sand. New friends parked up the hill on the street.

Ricardo and Mia approached quickly.

"We can't stay. Sorry. We're headed for Mia's mom's house for dinner. She's been down lately." He put his arm around Mia's shoulders. "Feeling sad."

Mia slipped her arm around his waist under his leather jacket. "We wanted to tell you and Professor Boyd in person."

Dani meandered up. "Tell me what?"

"We can't stay for dinner. Family obligation," Ricardo said. "We didn't want you to think we'd deserted you."

"Don't worry. Thanks to you two, I've met quite a few people. Cass will take care of me." She smiled. "Stay for a little bit and then sneak out when you need to."

"We'll catch you up on anything interesting that happens later," I said. "I'll give Sara a call after Jack and Gillian go back home. Maybe we can all get together and cheer her up a bit. It's been a while since we spoke."

"She'd like that," Mia said. "She misses you."

"Let's go in. It's a bit chilly out here." I led the way into the house but left the wooden door open.

As we entered, Ricardo scanned the room.

"She's not here yet," I said. "She never called back to let me know she wasn't coming, but with both you and Brendan here tonight, the odds are good Samantha won't come."

Jack silently handed Ricardo a beer. They exchanged a curt nod, and Ricardo took a long pull.

We all jumped when the screen door banged. I wasn't the only one who was tense.

Brendan walked in.

I smiled as Brendan scanned the room. "She's not here."

Brendan slipped out of his overcoat and hung it on my antique hall tree. "Not that I wouldn't be happy to see her."

"Of course."

Another knock.

"How many people did you invite?" Brendan asked.

"That's probably Phil, my ex."

Sure enough, Phil strutted in with Emily Beaton and Alice Wembly on each of his arms.

That didn't take him long. But it made sense, given that they were all staying at the Moon Coast Inn. They stopped in front of me.

"Welcome," I said and went through my drinks and food spiel.

"Thanks for inviting me." He handed me his coat.

"You're welcome." I hung his coat up on the hall tree. "You already know Jack and Gillian." I nodded toward Brendan. "Brendan's our local bookstore owner. Brendan, this is Phil, my ex-husband."

They shook hands.

Brendan whispered in my ear, "You're a brave woman." He wandered away.

Gotta love first impressions. I turned to Phil and smiled. "Let me introduce you to everyone else. Ricardo."

Ricardo raised a hand.

"And Mia." I scanned the room for George and Gillian but didn't see them.

Mia smiled at him. "Would you like something to drink?"

"Cocktails?" he asked with an upward lilt, telling me he was hopeful.

I cut in. "Sorry, no. Beer, hard cider, wine, or tea."

"I'll try a cider."

Mia went to fetch one.

"Dani, have you met Brendan yet?"

"I dropped by his bookstore. He's ordering a couple of local history and myth books for me."

Mia returned with Phil's cider as George joined us. "I hope you're not here on official business, George. Do you know Phil?"

"No, I'm here to cadge a free meal."

George and Phil shook hands.

"Aren't we all?" Brendan stroked his mustache, which was carefully groomed.

While he still looked like a portly Victorian professor with his waistcoat and pocket watch, his clothes were nattier than usual, no longer frayed around the edges. I thought I detected Samantha's hand in his wardrobe upgrade.

"I'll repeat this as people arrive. Jack and Gillian are acting as bartenders. Appetizers are set up around the first floor on various tables and the sideboard with small plates. We've laid two tables' worth of place settings, so sit wherever you want, including in the comfortable chairs in the living room, if you prefer. If everyone shows up, it'll be a full house. Tight quarters."

The group dispersed toward the appetizers, leaving me standing alone until Emily walked up to me.

"Isn't that the police officer?" she asked.

"Yes, he's the detective on the case, but he's also a friend of mine. We went to college together."

I looked over at George, who'd gotten a drink from Jack and was eyeing us. I wondered if he realized who Phil was. Phil and Alice joined us. He followed my gaze and stared at George. Then he looked at me with narrowed eyes. I smiled and tried to look innocent. I'm no actress, so I had no idea how good my attempt was.

Then he lifted his head slightly and smiled at Emily and Alice. "You two can stick with me. I'll protect you from the big, bad cop." Phil escorted them to the food tables.

If he was trying to make me jealous, it wasn't working.

Someone else knocked on the door, so I went to answer it.

"Samantha! Welcome." I stepped aside to let her in.

She breezed in looking a bit like a forest fire in flowing layers of red, orange, and yellow with a circlet of brassy yellow leaves crowning her wavy red hair. She paused and sized up the room.

"I wasn't sure I was coming, but then I thought what the hell." She waved her arms as she scanned the room. Her gaze lingered a moment on Brendan, who didn't turn around.

He must have heard her. Judging by the turned heads, everyone else did.

"I'm delighted to see you. It's been a while. I think there are only two new people for you to meet. Dani is a professor at the college, and," I inclined my head toward the fireplace, "my ex is holding court by the fire."

"Your ex?" She raised an exquisitely penciled auburn eyebrow. "This should be interesting."

I took her lovely emerald green coat and hung it on the hall tree. "I love the way this coat sets off your hair."

"That's why I bought it."

While many of Samantha's outfits were outlandish, tonight she was in full, voluptuous siren mode.

"Lovely dress. Would you like something to drink? White wine?"

"Perfect." Her eyes narrowed as she caught sight of Brendan, who now turned slightly in his chair, trying to see her without looking at her directly.

"I mentioned he was coming." I lowered my voice as the room had quieted.

"Yes, you did."

At the touch of steel in her voice, I scurried off to get her wine, passing through the scent cloud of her perfume. Mimosa? Perhaps it would take the edge off. When I returned, she was deep in conversation with Dani, and the two seemed to be hitting it off. I handed the glass to Samantha but kept still and listened.

One arched red eyebrow went up when she located Brendan again. This time their eyes met, and he blushed, the color creeping out from behind his whiskers. To me, the air seemed to crackle.

Dani strolled over to me as Ricardo came out of the kitchen with a glass of the cider. She lowered her voice. "Have I walked into a mare's nest?"

"Interesting expression," Ricardo said.

"I mean it in both senses of the phrase," Dani said. "The modern usage based on a misunderstanding of the old phrase. That definition would be that I've walked into a messy situation, and the—oh, about sixteenth century or so—meaning that someone here has seen something remarkable and as rare as a mare's nest or, more properly, a hoax because mare's nests don't exist. Or a chimera." She chuckled. "Or a ghost."

"For someone who studies folklore, you're a bit of

a skeptic."

Dani sipped her cider. "Actually, I'm an optimist. I keep finding hoaxes, but I'm always looking for the real things. And no, I don't believe in leprechauns."

"Stick around. You may see one yet."

Dani laughed and went to talk to Brendan. I wondered if she planned to talk books or flirt.

"Do you think Samantha has anything to worry about?" Gillian joined me, sipping her cider. "Men expect us to remain the same physically, emotionally, and mentally."

"It's as if they married a photograph, yet they get to put on weight, lose their hair, and quit trying to please us." I looked at Phil and thought about George.

"No wonder the marriage rate is dropping, and the murder rate is rising."

Why had Genevieve been murdered?

"Cass, are you all right?" Gillian frowned at me.

"I'm sorry. Did you ask me something?"

"You looked miles away." Gillian set her empty glass on the table. "Is there anything we can help with?"

I smiled. "I think it's time for dinner."

At a knock on my door, I turned. "Excuse me."

Tina stood on the other side of the screen door. I motioned for her to enter, and she timidly came over to us. Would she be able to run the company? Gen had been far more outgoing than her niece—a Siamese cat next to a brown mouse.

She slipped off her coat, her gaze darting around the room. She focused on Phil, Emily, and Alice. Then her body relaxed, and she smiled. Frank was dead. Who did she have to fear? Whoever it was, they weren't here at my dinner party.

Then she froze, and I glanced where she was looking. George stood in the kitchen door, a beer in his hand, looking at her. She walked over to him, and they both went into the kitchen. A moment later, Jack hurried out with an annoyed look on his face. He saw me and ambled over.

"I got kicked out of the kitchen before I could grab a beer."

"Did you catch what they were talking about?"

"You know George better than that. He didn't talk to her until I was out of earshot."

"Interesting."

Jack looked around the room. "Some folks are migrating to the two bigger tables. Phil has claimed the head of the dining room table with those two women from the genealogy competition on either side of him."

I nodded. "He's holding court. Samantha and Brendan are circling each other and the food, but I expect them to sit together."

"Where are Ricardo and Mia?"

"Last minute cancel. Family dinner. Sara's feeling lonely. After you guys leave, I'll spend some time with her. I think she really missed Alan over the holidays."

He nodded. "Do you want Gillian and me any place in particular? Balance out a group?"

"No, sit wherever you like." I smiled. "Keep your ears open. You could sit with Phil and eavesdrop on the two women."

He shook his head. "You are not sticking me with him. You'll have to do that yourself. I think I'll grab Gillian and sit over there." He pointed at the smaller table. "Tina and Dani have joined Brendan and, as you predicted, Samantha. Why don't you go find George? Bye." He headed toward Gillian.

I made my way to the stack of plates and, lured by the blended smells, gathered some succulent cabbage, dilled potatoes, corned beef, and soda bread and sat with Phil, Emily, and Alice. As I sat, I felt my chair being pushed in and looked up to see George, who leaned over and whispered in my ear, "Be right back."

His warm breath tingled against my cheek. A rush of gratitude washed over me.

"Hi, I'm Cass. Phil and I used to be married."

Chapter 20

"You'd be surprised at the mindsets of some criminals." George set his fork down. His hand brushed mine. "Excellent meal, by the way, Cass. You all may have seen a video that was posted years ago. I believe it was originally shown on one of those so-called reality shows. There's a riot, and one young man picks up a brick and hurls it at a store window. Good throwing arm. Should have gone into baseball. The brick bounces off the window and col—uh, hits him square in the forehead, knocking him out. He's still unconscious when the police lock him up."

"He sounds stupid," Phil said.

George shrugged. "He's just a victim of social learning. He learned from watching others in his neighborhood do smash and grabs. It never occurred to him that one poor store owner got tired of the cost of getting a professional glazer to redo his broken windows every time a mob smashed them and replaced the glass himself with an acrylic substitute."

Emily and Alice broke out in peals of laughter.

"Criminals are idiots," Phil said.

"Not necessarily. One very clever fellow wanted to get rid of his wife. He was good with his hands and had taken shop in school. His wife praised him for all the odd jobs he'd done around the house. He told us that during his interrogation for murder."

Emily sat up straight.

"He thought a divorce would cost him too much."

Phil snorted. "He was right there."

George ignored him. "So he repaired the deck that was off their bedroom three stories up. He said she told him she loved the pattern right before she stepped out on it and fell to her death."

"How?" Alice asked.

George smiled. "He was a very clever fellow. His wife loved jigsaw puzzles, so he created a giant puzzle for the floor of the deck. Beautiful and ingenious. One small problem. He didn't affix the pieces one to the other or to the joists. He laid them in place to show her what it would look like when it was finished. He said that he told her to wait until he'd reinforced it. His word against hers, and she was dead. It was more a case of not thinking through the consequences. He wasn't an idiot. He was too clever. I believe the charge was manslaughter, not murder."

Alice leaned forward. "What about the deaths here? The news says murder."

"We're still investigating."

Alice grimaced and leaned back. "That doesn't make us feel any safer. Several people have dropped out of the process to locate a guardian."

"In more ways than one," George said under his breath and looked at me.

Had people died that I didn't know about, or did he mean Frank, dropping off the cliff? "Why don't you stay after dinner to catch up?"

He smiled.

"I take it you're no closer to catching the murderer then," Phil said. "Cass seems to like to play Nancy

Drew. I saw a spreadsheet of suspects on her brother's computer."

A chill raced down my spine. I'd have to talk to Jack. If he hadn't shown it to him, then Phil had been snooping around my house.

"Are you sure she wasn't outlining a book? A murder mystery?" George asked.

"Cass can't write."

"Really? She's been remarkably helpful in our past investigations."

I flashed back to his telling me to stay out of the way and to leave it to the professionals. I thought I heard the faint echo of laughter, but it might have been someone from the other table.

George turned to me. His foot hit mine. "Tight quarters. In any case, I will stay after dinner. I'd like your opinion on a few matters."

"Of course. Glad to be of service."

"You two," he gestured at Emily and Alice, "you've been brave enough to stick around despite the danger you think you might be in."

"Does that make us suspects?" Alice asked, with a happy twinkle in her eye.

"Naturally," George said.

Alice and Emily looked at each other happily.

"You've been very helpful in our inquiries. But," George leaned toward them, "you might be the murderers, colluding in the crime and trying to perpetrate a fraud to gain an inheritance."

"Yes?" Alice bent toward him.

"Or you might be able to help me figure out whether or not Frank's death was an accident or…murder."

Emily patted her lips daintily and tucked her napkin under the side of her plate. "You said Frank dropped off the cliff. I thought he was going for help?"

"I can tell you a little bit about that because you'll probably hear it on the news or from your colleagues. Frank stopped on a side trail on the way out to talk to a woman who was part of the group. They were seen from a distance by a few members of your group who'd decided to stay behind and hike the park. They were up on a hill and thought they heard arguing below them. That's why they stopped to check it out, fortunately for us. Now, can you two tell me anything else?"

Phil frowned. His expression reminded me of all the times in the past when he no longer was the center of attention.

"What about me? Aren't I a suspect?" Phil asked.

George turned to him. "Do you want to be?"

Yes, yes, please.

"I have no motive."

"That I know of."

That seemed to shut him up.

George refocused on Emily and Alice. "Think back to that day in the state park. Look around. What do you see?"

Alice's gaze unfocused. "I looked down at the scavenger sheet Frank gave us to see what I should look for next. There was a picture of a mushroom that grows on trees. I looked, holding the sheet in front of me for comparison. Over the top, I saw Frank and Mrs. Wainwright talking about bats." She frowned. "But there weren't any bats. It was broad daylight. They wouldn't be out. I wondered if there was a cave nearby. He could have been warning her about rabid bats."

As she started speculating instead of stating what she'd actually seen and heard, George turned to Emily. "And you?"

"I was nearby, but I was searching for the fern in the picture above the mushrooms. Mrs. Wainwright's shoes were all wrong for a hike. I thought she was talking to him about her feet bothering her. Something about feet or foot. I focused on the picture again. Mrs. Wainwright screamed, and they weren't there anymore—"

Alice cut in. "I saw him put his arms up as if trying to catch his balance. He grabbed for her, but as she turned to try to save him, he fell."

"And a good thing, too," Emily said. "She's so tiny and in those shoes…" She shook her head. "If she'd succeeded in grabbing him, she'd have gone right over the edge with him."

"Did you see her after Frank fell?" George asked.

She furrowed her brow. "I don't remember seeing her after that. I was shocked and shoved the paper into my pocket."

"Did you, Alice?"

Alice shook her head. "No, but if Cass had invited her to this nice dinner, we could have asked her what happened."

Was that an accusation? I hadn't invited her, either. I'd invited Phil to be polite, and he'd brought the two women, which had seriously overstretched the space in my little bungalow. Someone else had said something about a bat, but I couldn't quite remember what it was.

"That nice Mr. Fochspaw isn't here, either, Emily."

Adrian Fochspaw from Frank's list. I hadn't met him, and no one else had mentioned him until now. But he was on the list for the hike. Gen had notes on him. Silver hair. Distinguished. Owned real estate. Divorced twice.

George's fingers curled as if he were itching to write something down. "What do you know about him?"

Emily giggled. "Silver fox."

"With a name that sounds like 'fox paw,' we've started referring to him as the silver fox. He has lovely silver hair. Longish. Thick. He's quite good looking. Owns property, I think," Alice said.

Phil frowned.

"Doesn't really seem the type to be the guardian for a cat," Emily said. "Too much cat hair on those impeccable suits."

"Suits?" George prompted.

Alice nodded. "Yes. All the time."

"Although he wore a safari outfit for the hike," Emily said.

"He did, but it was pressed. Khaki, knee socks, the whole nine yards."

"True," Emily said. "Perfect gentleman."

"What about Steve Simmons?" George asked.

"Young. College student, I think."

"Yes. Pre-law," Alice said. "He decided it wasn't for him, dropped out of the competition, and left."

"So, you two," George gestured between the women, "think of these proceedings as a competition?"

They both nodded.

"I wonder how many potentials decided not to come or didn't stay," I said, thinking back to Tina's flash drive and the deaths. "Or were prevented from coming."

"I'm sure the police have that covered," Phil said. "Ladies, how about a little dessert?"

Chapter 21

After everyone but George had left, Jack and Gillian cleared and got a load of dishes in the dishwasher. We all sat at the table in the dining room away from the noise of the sloshing water.

Jack opened his laptop to show George our spreadsheet. "We've missed you."

"Sorry about that. There's a lot going on. I'm up for promotion, so I've been trying to distance myself from certain controversial elements in my life." He raised an eyebrow at me. "However, I've decided that I can't fake my life to get a promotion, and they'll have to take me as I am or not at all. Rusty is in direct competition with me and has done a certain amount of undermining while also spending a lot of time with me and flattering me. As in any business, it's a bit of a political game."

Jack nodded. "Same thing where I work."

Remembering Phil's comment, I said, "Jack, did you show Phil the spreadsheet?"

"Of course not! How could you even think that?"

"He said he'd seen it during our conversation at dinner."

Jack looked at George. "That means that little weasel has been snooping around Cass' house. Can you arrest him?"

George laughed. "No, sorry. So, that's your ex-husband. He's quite good looking, if a little slippery, and, it seems, a hit with the ladies. If he were involved with this murder, he'd be at the top of my suspect list."

I was at a loss for a decent retort.

Fortunately, at that moment Gillian brought the electric kettle out to the dining room. "I'm not playing hostess and continuing to fill people's cups. This is get-it-yourself night. I'm already tired. For a while, I thought Samantha and Brendan were going to kill each other and give you another crime to solve, George, but they left together. Don't know if you noticed, Cass. I saw Phil give you a hard time right to the end."

"You do have lousy taste in men, Sis. Present company excepted."

"Thanks," George said dryly. "But why you preferred him over me, I'll never know."

"I was young and stupid. He was settled and in a safe profession."

"Says the lady who keeps finding corpses."

"Plus, you hurt my feelings when you didn't take my opinion on your going into law enforcement into consideration."

"By not doing what you wanted."

"Yeah." When he put it that way, it even sounded petty to my ears now although I'd felt rather self-righteous at the time.

He relaxed. "I'm glad you're no longer married to him."

"Me, too."

"I don't know how closely you've been following the news…"

"Silly question." Gillian filled her own cup and sat.

Jack tapped the computer screen he'd been trying

to show George.

"All right then. Hey!" George yelped as if he'd been stung by an irate scorpion. "Where'd you get this information?" He pulled Jack's computer closer.

"I asked politely," I said.

"We had to get a search warrant." He glared at me.

"You should come over more often. Seriously, you have to do that for chain of evidence for a court case. I, on the other hand, can snoop."

He grinned crookedly. "I guess you can be pretty handy to have around."

"Now you're getting the idea."

"Break it up, you two," Jack said. "We have work to do."

"Genevieve was a nice, honest woman," George said.

"I could have told you that just by meeting her." I put a dragon pearl jasmine tea bag in my cup and covered it with hot water. Mina would have been horrified, but it was late and I was too tired to prepare my tea properly.

"She may have solved her own murder with her meticulous notetaking and recordkeeping. We suspected a few people."

"I noticed you didn't sit at the same table as Dani, so I assume you no longer suspect her."

He nodded. "Your ex bringing two eyewitnesses to the party was quite a bonus. I'm very glad you decided to finally invite me. I was getting tired of waiting."

"Really?" I rested my chin on my palm, elbow on the table and stared at him.

He smiled, and his eyes closed halfway.

"Get a room!" Jack said.

I cleared my throat. "I like Frank or Phil for her murder," I said, but my heart was warm.

George shook his head. "I really see Phil more for the bounce-back brick type of crime."

I laughed.

"Did we miss something?" Jack asked.

"A story George told at dinner about types of criminals." I turned to George. "We could frame him."

"Vengeance is mine saith the ex-wife? Not sure I should get involved with you," George said.

"You *are* involved with me."

He kissed me.

"Again? Break it up! Okay, George, what was Frank's motive? The only one I see with a clear motive for both is Tina, particularly considering Frank's dead."

"But I like Tina!"

"Cass, you'll need a colder heart if you're going to keep trying to do my job. Now, let's assume that Tina has a secret. Let's also assume she wants something to happen and she's not willing to wait. She feels she waited long enough. There's only one obstacle in her way."

"How could she kill a woman who's been like a mother to her?" Gillian asked.

"For love."

"Tina's not in love!" I protested.

"Yes, she is, and she's up to her neck in fraud. She was trying to establish her boyfriend as the guardian; whereas, Frank was playing a longer game. Instead of a boyfriend he wanted to establish his mother, from whom he'd be the natural inheritor to be the next guardian. But Genevieve had uncovered both their games. Smart woman, but way too compassionate and trusting."

"How so?"

"She talked to each of them about what they'd done. Both had a motive to kill her, but it never occurred to her that one of them might murder her. One succeeded and then tried to wipe away all trace of the misdeed and throw shade onto the other one. Each learned the other's plans through Gen, but neither was the trusting sort. Their plans were at odds. Each wanted the fortune for themselves."

"Why did you suspect Dani, and don't say you didn't."

"I did. She was always acting suspiciously."

I remembered the Christmas tree. "But who killed all the other DNA relatives?" My eyes narrowed. "You haven't crossed her off your suspect list."

"Possibly." George leaned back and stared at me. "How do you know any other people were murdered?"

I hesitated. "Tina…"

"And after what I just told you?"

"Now I'm wondering if it was all a lie. But she couldn't have stolen the flash drive, and why would she have? She's the one who gave it to me in the first place. No, she has to be the innocent. She's being framed. One of the guardianship candidates?"

"Flash drive?" George's voice was quiet and very gentle, which put me on my guard. He'd always been most dangerous when he was quiet.

"I would have given it to you, but I seem to have lost it." I pivoted to Jack. "Or it was stolen?" I glanced back at George. "We thought Dani was the only one of the DNA relatives that had been in my house, but I don't always lock my doors." I shrugged. "Tina printed this out for me." I pushed the printout toward George. "She said it was on the flash drive. She provided me with a lot of information, which makes her seem more innocent to me."

"Unless she was lying to you and trying to mislead you."

"Why would she?"

"Does she know about our relationship? She could be trying to influence the investigation."

"True. Someone else who's been lurking in the shadows is this silver fox guy. Alice and Emily were quite taken with him, and yet I'm not even sure I met him. I was so busy taking pictures on the hike."

"You're just telling me now that you have pictures of a crime scene. Possibly two crime scenes, if Dani wasn't faking the whole asthma inhaler issue."

"How can you say she was faking a near-death experience?"

"How can you believe that everyone always tells you the truth?"

"I don't. People reveal themselves. I suspected Dani at first. Besides, you weren't exactly inviting confidences."

"Cass, do you understand that this is my job and that you have a responsibility to come forward with this kind of information...whether or not you and I are getting along?" He sighed. "Look. What makes this information suspect is that Tina gave it to you instead of us. Why?"

"It's for her website."

"Information about a possible mass murder is for her website? Think about it."

I felt like an idiot. I liked Tina and I hadn't

questioned her motives. I didn't even think she had motives. She'd just inherited total control over a lucrative company. Maybe he was right, and I wasn't cut out for this.

"We know Frank used his position with the company to identify his competition," George said. He flipped through the pages. "This confirms several things. May I take it with me?"

I couldn't refuse. "Be my guest. I've already scanned it."

George chuckled ruefully. "Of course, you have." He stood. "On that note, I'll take my leave of you all. Delightful party. Delicious dinner, as always."

On the verge of tears, I walked him to the door, but he took me by the hand at the threshold, pulled me through the doorway, and stepped into the shadows, taking me with him. As he held me, something heavy dropped into my pocket.

"Don't say I never do anything for you," he whispered as he gently kissed my cheek.

As he walked out to his car, I realized how much I'd missed him.

I slipped my hand into my pocket and felt the familiar shape. I pulled my cell out and texted him a string of hearts.

Chapter 22

Saturday morning, I got up late after tossing and turning and having nightmares about silver-haired men and dead bodies. I dressed slowly, listening for sounds of movement downstairs. I'd have to wait to shower until they were up; otherwise, I'd wake them. By the time I went down, I heard the shower. Today would be a slow, lazy day after the excitement of last night…or so I thought.

Doris popped out of my fridge. "You all really have no idea how to do a séance properly. You have to raise the energy level within the circle. You're not providing enough energy for the spirits to be able to manifest, to move things, to get through to you."

"Why were you in my fridge?"

"Checking to see what you have for breakfast before Mina gets here."

"Why is Mina coming here?"

"Oh, didn't I say? She wasn't at the party last night."

"I noticed."

"She had an issue with Missy and Prissy."

"I already know I won't be able to follow this conversation without caffeine." I proceeded to make a lot of coffee, knowing that Jack and Gillian had been imbibing pretty heavily the night before.

"But—"

I held up a hand.

She shrugged and tapped her long, purple fingernails on my countertop until I yelled, "What?"

Jack walked into the kitchen, towel-drying his hair. "I didn't say anything."

I turned around. Doris had vanished.

"Can I bang my head on the wall for a while?"

"Be my guest." He sat at the table. "Coffee ready?"

The only thing preventing me from strangling my little brother was the knock at the door, followed by Gillian's yell.

"I'll get it!"

He picked up my phone that was charging on the counter. "When did you get this back?"

"Last night."

Before I could say more, Gillian and Mina entered the kitchen. Without a word, Mina handed me a tin of lemon bars. I took them. "What did I do to deserve this?"

"It's by way of apology for missing your party last night."

I shrugged. "I appreciate that you gave up your place so that I could squeeze George in, which turned out to be unexpectedly delightful, by the way. My ex brought two plus ones, so we already had one person more than my little place can hold comfortably."

"Speaking of unexpected beings showing up, Missy and Prissy paid me a visit last night. I had some difficulty without Doris' help in understanding what they wanted."

Imagined head slap. "I'm so sorry, Mina. The ghost cat totally rolled off my to-do list. Let me just drink this." I returned to fixing a cup of coffee.

Mina let me drink half a cup before she asked, "Do you think we could hold a séance today?"

So that's what Doris was alluding to.

"We've done past séances in my loft, but Prissy has been showing up over at your place. We could hold a séance over there to see if we can communicate with her."

Doris rejoined us with a snap and raised one perfectly penciled eyebrow. "Just how are you planning to communicate with a cat? Meow much?"

"See, that's where you come in."

Her eyes widened.

I hurried on. "I thought you could inhabit Thor again and…talk to Prissy."

"Oh, you did, did you?"

"There will be shrimp…"

Mina knew how to lure a cat…or cat inhabitor, in this case. It was the only way a ghost could enjoy shrimp.

I set out honey, sugar, and milk. "Let's see. Where are those lemon bars?" I took the lid off the container and set it on the table. "We might as well have sweets with our tea."

When everyone's cup was filled, I sat. "Where does that leave us? We had a dinner party. I have to finish up a couple of projects for the company. I have zero idea where I stand with George, but after Doris possessed him…" I shook my head.

"Yeah, that's a relationship ender." Jack bit into a lemon bar.

"I'm afraid he's right, Cass," Mina said. "The look on his face. Eyes wide. Mouth open. He staggered. The only way I can describe it is world ending. For him, it was an apocalypse."

I sighed. "I was probably kidding myself. He's the kind of guy who likes his life with neatly hemmed edges or, in my case, hedges…between us."

"Whereas you have no borders, edged, hedged, or otherwise." Jack sipped his tea. "Ow. Hot."

"But he did come last night." And there was that moment between us in the semi-darkness.

"Speaking of which, what was George getting at after dinner?" Gillian blew on her tea. "Were there two murders or two accidents at the park? Why is Dani's name underlined in George's notes if these are only accidents? Is something else going on?"

"All good questions," I said. "I wish I knew. There isn't enough info to make a guess."

"Although both you and George made several." Jack set his cup down. "Sometimes patterns can arise from chaos."Gillian reached over and patted my hand. "Cass, I don't think there's anything there. All smoke; no fire. What if Gen's death was a random mugging and Frank's an accident?"

"And Dani didn't keep track of her inhaler usage? I've never used one, but isn't there a counter on the doohickey?" I asked.

"Doohickey?"

"Jack, slight change of subject. I added the data from the hike into the spreadsheet."

Jack rolled his eyes.

"At least have a look."

He went over to the dining room table and opened his laptop.

"Did you upload the photos? You were using digital cameras," Gillian said.

Mina's eyes smiled at me over the rim of her teacup. "Does this mean you might have time to work on my little problem?"

I'd totally forgotten about my mission to find out Prissy's purpose. "I'll consult with Doris, and we'll get back on your project."

Mina set her cup back in its saucer and rose. "In that case, I'll take myself back home. Let me know what you find out."

"Will do." I walked her to the door. "Thanks for your help."

She waved as she ambled up the path.

When I got back to the kitchen, Gillian had already cleaned up.

She hung the towel to dry. "I'm not forgetting Genevieve. I'm just saying that dead bodies don't always mean murder."

"Gillian, I love your positive outlook, but she was injected with drugs. That takes planning. Can we at least agree that there's been a murder? I believe that the deaths are connected, so I'm a tad suspicious. George asked questions last night that lead me to believe that Frank's mother is also dead. Emily and Alice had slightly different answers to his questions, but one of them said that both Frank and his mother disappeared." I held up a hand to forestall any argument. "However, are those peas for dinner tonight? They won't shell themselves."

George had mentioned a few other participants who saw Frank from a different angle. I hoped Dani could find out who they were.

I pulled out a lined trash can for the shells and two bowls for the peas.

"You're not throwing out the pods, are you?"

"Believe it or not, I've started composting."

"That's great!"

"I figure I can grow my own peas, tomatoes, kohlrabi, peppers."

Jack brought his computer and joined us. "It was getting lonely out there."

"Your timing is excellent. Do you think you can knock together a couple of raised bed boxes out back before the end of the weekend?" I asked.

Gillian shelled a pod, and deposited the pod in the bin. "Your sister is composting."

"Sure. Happy to." He turned the laptop screen toward us. "I looked at the data you entered, set up a cloud link between our two machines, and I've got a link to the spreadsheet set on both laptops. I think, despite my wife's skepticism, that we should consider that we have three murders. That way we won't miss anything."

"I agree," I said. "Although I think there were three murders and an attempt on Dani. It feels like an iceberg to me. There's more below the surface that we can't see."

Gillian opened her mouth but shut it again. "Okay."

I read the screen. "Wait a minute. You have Dani listed as an intended victim and a suspect."

"Please note that at this point the suspect list is very long. Every person who expects to inherit must be considered a suspect. I think you're forgetting that an attempt was made on Dani's life. Her inhaler?"

"True, but from what Doris saw, the police considered her a suspect." I scratched my nose. "But last night, George…"

Gillian said, "We don't know that for sure. Maybe they've highlighted her as the next victim."

"But Frank tried to kill her, didn't he? And now he's dead."

Chapter 23

"Maybe the notes Doris saw were written before he did. We haven't seen the context. Maybe what George said was true, and they moved on to the next suspect."

"Context." I wondered if we had missed the bigger picture. "What is the context for Genevieve's murder? Seems to me she was helping all these people. Why would they want to kill her?"

Gillian shook her head. "She must have uncovered something that someone didn't want brought to light."

"Now, did you find that flash drive that Tina gave me?" I looked around. "Rats. We've cleaned the place a little too well."

"You think Tina might have included something that would be a clue to Genevieve's murder?"

I shrugged. "Frank was angry with her for giving us whatever was on it. It's here somewhere." I looked around.

"We'll find it," Gillian said. "We won't leave until Sunday. We'll have the whole weekend to find it if we don't run into it before that."

"I feel uncomfortable not having it tucked away before we had company here."

Jack laughed. "We probably have already tucked it away."

"True," I said. "Let's finish up the peas."

****

After lunch, I called Mina, and we headed over to try to communicate with Prissy. Our pace was slow to accommodate Thoris. Despite Doris' best efforts, Thor was easily distracted by butterflies as he trotted up the hill to Mina's. I offered to use my cat carrier, but Doris preferred to use Thor as transport.

Mina's formal parlor was too small for six of us to sit in a circle on the floor, so we decided to use her bedroom. Prissy had manifested there at the foot of her bed. But nothing happened. Meowing, Thoris wandered all over the house, from the attic to the mouse-ridden basement. We finally had to send Jack down to scoop Thoris up, carry them up the stairs, and lock the door. Thoris staggered a few steps, fell over, and snored sonorously.

"Mina, may we borrow your cat carrier?" I asked.

"Of course. I'm so sorry. I have no idea what the problem is."

"When I get Thoris home and Doris can leave Thor again, I'll ask if she has any idea and get back to you."

"Thank you for trying."

Back home, the minute we got in the door, Doris fell out of Thor, who continued sleeping. I put the carrier in the living room with the side unzipped so that he could get out when he woke up.

Doris staggered sideways across the room and fell over, half in and out of the floor. "That cat is a maniac!"

"Are you all right?"

"I'm so dizzy I can't see straight." She vanished.

"Thor had the zoomies," Gillian said.

"Does anyone know why cats zip around like that?" I asked.

"Cats," Gillian said as if that explained it.

****

I'd noticed faint scratching and distant cats meowing. But the sounds hadn't moved from my subconscious to my conscious mind until now, when the meowing became an avalanche: the thunderous meowing of a thousand cats, threatening to sweep me down a mountain of noise and bury me in their insistent pleading.

"I can't stand it!"

Jack jumped up. "What?" He looked around for the source of my anguished cry.

"Can't you hear them?"

He narrowed his eyes. "Hear what?"

Clearly, he thought I was losing it because he didn't hear them. I wasn't the only one who did, though. Doris popped in, covering her ears.

"You have to do something. Make them stop!"

Gillian walked in from the porch. "Stop what?"

"That incessant meowing!"

"We can't put it off any longer. We have to have that séance here and now. Doris, we'll need Thoris. Gillian, can you get Mina? Tell her we have to contact Prissy and the spirit cat. Whatever they want, it's reached a crescendo."

Gillian nodded and dashed out the front door.

"Jack, I'll need help prepping the loft. I guess it will only be us. Anyone else would think we're nuts."

Jack stood. "You realize that this will be a real séance, and for the first time, you won't be able to understand what the ghost wants."

I sighed. It had occurred to me. "That's why we'll need Thoris."

Doris took her cue and vanished to find Thor. Jack headed upstairs, and I waited for Gillian and Mina. We wouldn't need the trappings we used for human séances when setting the mood was all important. These ghosts weren't concerned with atmosphere. No idea what was going to happen. Fifteen minutes later, Gillian returned with Mina carrying a large satchel.

Mina patted my arm. "I've been hearing them all morning, too. Their cries have echoed up the hill, so I'm prepared. Shall we go?"

Gillian went up first, reaching down to help Mina climb the last few steps, which were harder even though the railing extended above the floor, a precaution I'd taken to avoid falling in the middle of the night. Having a circular hole in the middle of the floor of my bedroom had freaked me out ever since I'd moved in.

I followed them upstairs.

Jack had laid out four cushions on the floor at the compass points. He hadn't gotten the Ouija board out, but he had placed the low table in the center with a candle. A small bag of catnip sat next to the candle.

Mina seated herself and picked up the catnip to stuff it into her bag. "Thoughtful, but I think that might be more of a distraction." She moved the candle aside and pulled a large, folded piece of paper from her capacious bag. After unfolding it, she patted it flat.

I sat next to her for a closer look. It was a floor plan of the old mansion.

I must have nodded because Mina smiled and said, "You see what I'm going for, don't you?"

"I wondered how we were going to exchange information. Doris will inhabit Thor and become Thoris, but we already know that cat-slash-human

179

communication is iffy at best. Either you instinctively know what an animal wants or you don't."

"Too bad we don't have one of those word button boards they use with dogs," Jack said.

"I wouldn't be too sure that the dog knows what it's saying. It's definitely stimulus response. The dog hits a certain button randomly, and the owner gets its leash and takes it for a walk. When the dog wants a walk, it hits a button. This time it gets a treat. Slowly, it learns how to control its owner's behavior. The dog is learning how to train its owner to do what it wants. Meanwhile, the owner thinks he's established meaningful communication with his dog. We need to think like the cat."

"That's why I brought the catnip," Jack said.

I shook my head. "That'll just make Thor loopy."

He shrugged. "What do you think we should do?"

I looked up at Jack. "Can you run back downstairs, turn off the lights so that no ambient light comes up through the floor, and then turn off the lights up here. Then, I guess, we'll be winging it."

Moments later, all four of us were seated around the floor plan. Mina lit the candle with her purple electric candle lighter. We held hands as a large, furry, shadow joined us, sitting between Mina and me.

Mina spoke. "Hello, Prissy. You know me and you know the spectral guardian. I ask you to be the link between us to help us find out what we must do to give her peace."

We waited. Thoris purred. That surprised me. I was more used to Thor grumbling.

A pale pink glow suffused the loft. At first, I thought I imagined it. The gleam didn't light the room.

On the contrary, the glow was more of a mist than a radiance.

Mina shifted and nodded her head. "The guardian of the diary."

Diary? Not treasure? I reached into my pocket and flicked the ringer off with my thumb nail. Whatever this was, I didn't want to disturb it.

The paper on the table crinkled as if touched by an invisible finger. In this case, probably a paw. The effect was of something small and invisible, moving from room to room as if looking for something. Then it stopped. Five holes appeared in the paper along with a tiny sixth. The holes encircled a junction in a wall between two walls and the edge of the fireplace in the library.

I bit my tongue to keep from exclaiming.

"Thank you. The diary is in the wall by the fireplace in the library," Mina whispered.

After her counterpoint about the word button board, I was surprised that she verbalized in English an exact location. But who was I to question her methods? Mina was her own mystery, and as they say, there was method to her madness.

A bright light appeared in the upper corner of the loft. The hazy outline of a cat floated into the light that winked out behind it. Thoris purred again.

I looked down on him or her, but didn't move. I had a million questions. What diary? Why was Thoris purring? What, if anything, was Mina picking up from the ether or the ghost cat? Was I hallucinating?

A breeze blew the candle out, and we plunged into darkness.

Chapter 24

I felt Thoris get up and shake. I heard a grumpy groan, and Thor thumped down the circular staircase.

"Doris?" I whispered.

"You can turn on the lights," Mina said. "I believe we have our answer."

Jack yelped and swore but managed to find the switch.. "Okay, so… Did anyone get anything out of that?"

"Yeah," Doris said, arms crossed over her chest. "A cat gets to go into the light. What is this? A cat! Where's *my* light? We solved my murder, and I didn't go into the light. Now I have to find my purpose and accomplish it to go into the light? What else is in the fine print?"

"Doris, dear," Mina said gently. "The guardian of the diary fulfilled her purpose. It was time for her to go into the light."

"Haven't I fulfilled my purpose?"

"I don't know, dear. Have you?"

"How should I know what my purpose is?"

"Then, dear, my guess is that you haven't yet fulfilled it."

Doris disappeared in a sickly lime green cloud.

"That was just nasty," Jack said.

"Mina, what happened? What do you know?" I stacked the cushions in the corner.

"I've been in the mansion a number of times. I have a mental map of it. As the guardian walked across the floor plan, I saw the rooms and watched as she—"

"She?"

"Yes. It's my impression. I also felt that she became non-gendered when she passed over." Mina tilted her head. "I don't know that for sure."

I nodded. "Sorry for the interruption."

"She paused at the fireplace and raised her paw. I believe I can locate the area with some certainty. We need permission to go and search. The police have been oddly silent about this case."

In more ways than one. I'd felt the ache of George's absence, but remembered the lash of his anger and then the warmth of his kiss last night. These mood shifts were so unlike him. What was going on?

"But the cat left."

Mina nodded. "Her duty was to guard the location of the diary until it was time to reveal it. I think the changes in guardianship of the estate and the current cat indicated that it was time that whatever is in that diary should be revealed. Once she'd dispatched her mission, it was time to go."

"Doris is really mad."

Mina smiled. "Doris' mission is not yet complete."

"But she doesn't even know what it is."

"She will. She also knows the location of the diary, and she might also have more details…when she calms down."

"Poor thing," Gillian said. "I wonder what her purpose is?"

"If it's to scare the crap out of me, she's already achieved her purpose," I said. "Several times over."

****

Mina had taken her cat carrier with her and gone home. We were preparing lunch when George dropped by. I was delighted to see him again. It felt like old times, but I still felt uncertain of where I stood. The four of us sat around the trestle table in the kitchen, munching sandwiches, olives, and pickles and discussing the cat séance and the diary that Mina was hoping to find at the mansion.

"What is it with you and séances?" George said between bites.

"Most of it is flummery."

"Flummery?"

"I was looking for a new dessert and ran into Flummery, a soft pudding, but I remembered my grandmother using the word in a totally different context. So, I looked it up. It also means 'Meaningless or deceptive language; humbug.' If you use a word three times in context, it sticks with you…usually."

"I see. I look forward to the dessert. Not so much the deceptive language. You were making it up as you went. Got it. But with the cat, you think…"

"There was a bright light, and a shadowy cat floated into it, so, yes. Also, Doris was very pissed that she didn't get to go into the light. She thought it was real, and I'm inclined to believe her since she is a ghost."

"I'm sorry you didn't invite me. This one sounds like fun."

"I'll remember you said that next time."

"Next time?"

A knock on the door made us all, with the exception of George, jerk involuntarily.

"A bit jumpy?" George raised an eyebrow. "Expecting Phil?"

"Don't even joke about it." I opened the door to a shivering Dani.

"Sorry, came out without my jacket. It's colder than I expected here on the coast. I've looked everywhere else, but I must have left my phone here. Can't find it anywhere. Don't have a landline to call it to see if it's between cushions. I came over on the chance you either found it or were still cleaning up and hadn't discovered it yet."

I closed the door behind her.

She looked at the group at the table with the computer open. "Sorry to interrupt. What's going on?"

"George is right. You really do act suspiciously," I said.

"Me?"

"You. In movies, people leave things behind intentionally so that they can go back to snoop. Go look for your phone and then join us. I have a few questions for you." I sat back down. "Speaking of phones, thanks for giving mine back. I was so lost without it. However, there was—"

He reached into his pocket, pulled a case out, and slid it across the table toward me.

I picked it up and snapped it on my phone. "Oh, baby, now you're whole again."

"Got it! And a lot of other stuff." Dani took the couch cushions off and piled them on the floor. "You might want to consider vacuuming under the cushions occasionally. If I took all this loot home, I'd be a rich woman."

We gathered around to see what she'd unearthed.

Dani picked up her phone. Jack made a dive for the cash. George reached for the flash drive.

Gillian removed the cat toys. "Thor's stash is no longer a secret."

I held out my hand, but George pulled out a baggie and slipped it inside.

"Really?"

"Dani, you had an extra inhaler on you during the hike at the state park. Why?"

She looked around at all of us. "Why wouldn't I? I have a life-threatening illness. Whoever wouldn't have a backup inhaler with them?"

"I wouldn't have," I said.

"Are you sure? Do you have a life-threatening illness? Have you ever felt so short of breath that you thought you'd suffocate at any moment?"

I looked down. "No."

"Walk a mile in my shoes." She'd set her bag on the floor next to her when she sat. She picked it up now and placed it on the table, pulling out two inhalers, an auto-injector that contained epinephrine, and a small first aid kit. "I can also do CPR and have certification. When your life depends on these things or help from other people, you learn how to survive and how to help other people." She picked up the epinephrine and held it out. "I don't need this for myself, but I've helped others with this. I've also given my spare inhaler to other asthma sufferers who weren't prepared. I don't kill people. I try to help others survive when I can."

Her voice was harsh, and I saw tears in her eyes and wondered if she'd lost someone.

"At the park, I couldn't get enough breath to tell them with everyone fussing around that I had a second inhaler. When they cleared out to get help, I was able to calm myself enough to get the second inhaler out of my backpack. It's very much about not panicking."

"Did you fake the asthma attack?" I asked.

Dani turned to George. "What did your lab find out?"

"The first one was empty, and the second canister nearly full," he said.

"So, that bears out what I said; however, you can also think that I emptied the first myself, faked the attack, and used the second so that the police would get the results I wanted." She turned to George. "You still suspect me, so you must have considered that angle. Doesn't matter now." She pulled an envelope from her bag. "I checked my mailbox on the way home." She opened the letter and handed it to George. "So, arrest me now if you're going to. This day couldn't get any worse."

Gillian got her a box of tissues. Dani blew her nose. George handed me the letter.

I scanned it. "Oh, no." I handed it back to her.

"Too bad this happened when I found someone I thought was a friend who'd help me bury a body."

George stiffened. "Is there something you'd like to tell me?"

Dani and I exchanged a glance.

"Relax, George. It's a metaphor." I turned to Dani. "Can you fight this?"

She shook her head. "No, I signed a one-year contract. That says they're not renewing it. That's their prerogative." She put her hand on my arm. "Don't worry about me. I've already applied for other positions locally. I can also probably find some adjunct teaching at local community colleges. I've done it before. Housing may prove more difficult. I'm renting from the university. I'd really like to find a home somewhere. I thought this was it, but no."

"I'm so sorry."

"Even though I always act suspiciously?"

"That would be half the fun. Besides, I like the way your mind works."

"I don't know if I can deal with two of you," George said. "Bad enough when Cass pokes around in my cases."

She waved her phone. "And before you ask, no, I hadn't left this behind on purpose to record your conversation after I left."

I started, remembering how I'd recorded Frank's words. Dani rolled her eyes.

Jack laughed. "Good one,"

"You don't suppose…," I said.

George held up his cell phone. "See this app? I always sweep when I walk into your house."

"Sweep?"

"This app lets me know if I'm being surveilled."

"You don't trust me?"

"No, I don't trust the people you piss off."

"I think I'm about to piss off another one." I looked at Dani. "A few days ago, I mentioned blackmail in your presence. I couldn't help noticing your reaction. Are you being blackmailed?"

She hesitated and looked at George. "I suppose it doesn't matter anymore." She took a deep breath. "Frank dug up some dirt on me and a student of mine. Bear in mind that I teach at the college level, so no hanky-panky with underage students. Anyway, he threatened to tell the college unless I dropped out of the competition."

"That's why you were less actively involved after the hike."

"That and nearly dying have a dampening effect on my enthusiasm." She ate half her sandwich.

Gillian passed her the bowl of multi-grain chips. Dani took a handful and then held up one chip.

"Are we just sojourners on a teensy planet in the unknown or unknowable? Is there a purpose to all of this?"

"You know there are ghosts, so there must be something else. Pass the chips," I said.

"I know there's something out there because beer exists." Jack went to the fridge. "George, want a beer?"

"Love one."

"Me, too," Dani said.

"I knew I liked you." Jack handed her an India pale ale.

She took it. "Sometimes I feel alone and that's when I wonder what it's all about."

"And that is exactly why we need to be kind to each other, to treat each other the way we want to be treated, and that's why you're coming over tomorrow and having Sunday dinner with us because when I'm feeling alone, I'd want a friend to be there for me. We're having spaghetti and amazing garlic bread," I said.

"You know, we work better together." Dani took a swig.

"Yes, we do."

Dani set her bottle down. "I hate to be a downer, but what are you going to do about Phil?"

"Drown him? Oops. Sorry, George. Guess that's the wrong thing to say in front of a detective."

"Oh, don't mind me." He took a swig and winked. "I've had the same thought."

Everyone laughed.

"The thing is, I can't let Phil see how much he upsets me. For him it would be a win. He's trying to be difficult to get back at me because I didn't welcome him with open arms. Now he's trying to score points. But I'm not sure he even knows why. For him to make me feel lesser is like he's scoring; he's making a basket. My best solution to dealing with him is simply to realize that this is what he does and not react the way he expects me to. I do have a kneejerk response to his jibes, but I am learning. It takes time and a lot of effort, and right now it's very disconcerting. I think I'm over it. I can walk away. I can find my own peace, my own calm. He still can get to me in the moment, but not in the long run." I glanced over at George.

"I'm really sorry I can't arrest him for you, Cass."

"Thanks. I appreciate the thought. I want him to leave before Jack and Gillian do."

"You do have a ghost," Dani said. "Have you thought about using her to get rid of Phil?"

"Please do not mention Doris to him."

"Why not? You don't seem to be using her to full advantage," Dani said.

"Don't get me started on how Cass uses her ghost," George said.

I had a thought that seemed significant, but as I tried to bring it into focus, it faded away. I hate that feeling that something brilliant is just out of reach. I let it go.

"Phil would find a way to monetize her to his advantage and my detriment. No, thank you."

Doris popped in on the countertop.

Dani shrieked, recovered herself, and said, "See what I mean? She could get rid of him."

"I'm happy to try." Doris morphed into something truly horrible.

"Doris! Please! We've just eaten." I covered my eyes.

She changed into something resembling a Twenties' actress with spit curls plastered to her head. "Better? I dropped by to tell you that I really appreciated everyone's help in getting me out of jail. I've already thanked Mina." She glared at George.

He raised his hands in surrender. "Be fair. I didn't lock you up."

Thor wandered in, sat back on his haunches, and pawed the air.

"That's my signal. He's hungry." I opened his tuna-flavored cat food.

"You know he's always aware of you, where you are in the house, and what you're doing," Doris said.

"Really?" I set his food bowl on the floor. "That's amazing." I patted Thor. "What a pretty and talented boy you are!"

He stopped eating, looked up at me, and meowed.

"I love you, too, sweetie." I turned around to see everyone staring at me. "What? Haven't you ever seen a crazy cat lady before?"

"Enough staring, everyone," Gillian said. "Is there anything you can tell us, George? These murders weren't sensational enough to get much coverage on the news."

"We've played it pretty close, providing just enough information to make it seem boring and humdrum."

"You've outdone yourselves," Jack said.

"I can tell you that Gen's computer was destroyed. IT restored it from backup."

"Brilliant!" I said. "Anything notable?"

"She had a gardening folder that we didn't pay any attention to until Tina told us that she wasn't an outdoor person and didn't garden. Then we went over it with a fine-toothed comb. There were photos, videos, and notes in the folder about each of the relatives, their relationships, and wrongdoings. There's a video of two of them in the back of a hay wagon. It's labeled "Italy" with a question mark. We've spent a lot of time on the data Gen collected. She was amazingly in-depth."

"I know," I said. "I really wanted to work with her."

"You're telling us this in front of Dani, so I take it she really is no longer a suspect," Gillian said.

"Everyone is a suspect until the case is closed and tied with a neat bow. Consider that I might be trying to get Ms. Boyd to make an unguarded statement."

Dani laughed. "All my statements tend to be unguarded. That's what always gets me into trouble."

George leaned back, raised both eyebrows as if questioning her statement, and finished his beer.

Dani frowned and squirmed. "Thanks for lunch and my phone. I'm going to head home. If the invite is still open, I'll see you for supper tomorrow."

"I'll show you out." I got up and walked her to the door. "Don't let George worry you." I paused. "Unless you're guilty." I opened the door.

She hugged me and left.

I watched her go before returning to the kitchen to clear the plates.

Chapter 25

"I didn't want to say this in front of Dani."

I set the plates in the sink and turned around. George was looking at me.

"It wasn't until Doris possessed me, that I realized that I had you all wrong. We shared some feelings and thoughts," George said.

"Like a Vulcan mind meld?" Jack said.

"In a way, but with plenty of emotion. You know your ghost; no holds barred."

That was true.

"So, what does this mean?" I held my breath.

"It means that I get it." George got up, put his hands on my upper arms, and stared into my eyes. "It means that my muddled feelings are now clear. I believe you care for me as me. Maybe even love me. I no longer think you were only using me in your sometimes bizarre…"

But I no longer heard him. I floated, untethered in time and space. With his words, the pattern fell into place, and I finally understood.

I refocused on George, who seemed to be expecting me to say something, so I did. "It *was* out of love. You arrested the wrong person."

"What?" His head jerked back.

"Did you hear what he asked you?" Gillian said.

I pulled out of his grasp. "We have to get them all

together. I'm still not sure of the details."

"Of the wedding?" Gillian asked.

"Does that mean you will?" George asked.

Doris floated by. "It means she solved the murders."

"Can you get Tina out of jail for this?" I asked George.

****

Three hours later, I'd filled a few people in on my idea, and we were all together in my living room: Tina, Adrian, Dani, George, Jack, Gillian, me, Mina, Emily, Alice, Phil, and Bill, who stood with his back against the front door. He had a cup of coffee in his hand, and a quirky smile on his face. I hadn't liked him when I'd first met him, but he had George's back in my little scheme, so I was warming to him.

Detective Rusty Riordan was outside with several officers, protesting, "This is not how we do things in Las Lunas. We have several perfectly good interrogation rooms down at the station. This is going to cost you, George."

"Thanks for coming," I said to everyone in my living room.

"Like we had a choice," Phil said.

"I had an epiphany while George was proposing—"

Jack laughed.

"What?" Phil said.

"I realized that this case has been a muddle from the beginning because, rather than too few motives, there were too many. However, once I figured out the pattern, it became clear."

"As mud," Phil said.

I really wanted to tell the peanut gallery to shut up, but he was revealing his character with every comment and cutting the strings that had still bound me to him.

"Everyone here—in fact, I'd say everyone here plus those at my party—was using someone or something else to further their own ambitions or," I looked at Phil, "needs."

I turned to George. "You were partially right. I did see you as a source of information, but that didn't mean that I wasn't falling in love with you all over again." I thought I heard Phil growl, but that could have been my stomach. "So, in a sense, I used you just as you used me." When I'd explained what I meant to do, he'd protested but understood our relationship now.

"And you, Phil. I won't go into detail on how and why you used me. Suffice it to say, you came here to try to use me again to see to your needs while you sought another girlfriend. *Tsk, tsk.*" I shook a finger at him as he tried to protest.

"Emily and Alice." I smiled. "You two used Phil mercilessly."

Phil stared at them.

"Caught in the act," Alice said.

"What?" Phil said.

"They used you, Phil, and your connection to me and my connection to George and Tina to try to find out who might win the competition. And," I swung a finger between the two of them. "You were also using each other. I have a suggestion. Mina is here as a representative of the Arts and History Commission of Las Lunas. She made an interesting find over at the mansion yesterday after she used me to gather some information in an unusual way."

She nodded. "Guilty as charged."

"We talked to the committee, and everyone thinks the two of you work well together and would make great joint guardians. I believe the cats, er, cat will also approve the choice."

Adrian stood. "Then I might as well leave if the choice has been made."

Bill moved to block the door.

"Not so fast, Adrian." I tapped my cheek with a forefinger. "Who might you have been using?" I looked at Tina. "You're a strikingly handsome man. I believe Alice and Emily referred to you as a 'silver fox.' Yet, you appear to be attracted to Tina, who is on the mousy side—sorry, Tina—and was recently arrested for the murder of her aunt."

"I don't know what you're talking about," he said huffily.

I noted Tina's expression. "I'll bet Tina does. Feeling a bit used, Tina?"

She nodded her head sullenly.

"And who did you use, Tina? Obviously, Adrian for pleasure. Can't blame you there. Frank. You were spying on Frank. The police found the location device you planted on him. You also used your kind aunt and even me. You played on my sympathies. You were oh so helpful with all that information you gave me that clearly pointed to Frank as the murderer. That would have gotten him out of the way. Someone ruined your plans by killing him."

She exhaled and drew her eyebrows together.

"No, it wasn't you. His killer messed up your plans, but you and Adrian are guilty of fraud. You're also guilty of embezzlement, so you'll be going back to jail."

Adrian looked quickly at the doors and windows.

"Don't bother, Adrian. There are officers outside, waiting to take you and Tina down to the station." I turned to George. "I loved saying that."

He laughed. "Don't lose the moment, you amateur."

Bill stifled a chuckle.

I thought I heard Phil mutter under his breath.

"Let's see. Who's left? We know Jack and Gillian use me as a cheap B and B."

"And for entertainment," Jack called out.

"Dani. You used your students, Mia and Ricardo, to get close to me. They'd opened up to you, and you are a natural observer and researcher. You used me to gather information."

"And nearly to help me bury a body."

I saw George stiffen out of the corner of my eye. "Relax, George. It's a little inside joke. I'll tell you the whole story later." I turned back to Dani. "Well, it worked. You got your info, but I hope we're friends. That's the upside of using people. If it's gentle and not too selfish, it can end up being a boon to both sides." I scanned everyone. "But being used can poison even a mother's love and turn it toxic. You may have noticed Mrs. Wainwright is strangely absent as are two other DNA relatives who were on the hike. There was no need for the other relatives to be here as they have dropped out of the competition and given their statements to the police, which provided the final bit of information about the other missing person, Frank's mother, Mrs. Wainwright."

A murmur went around the room.

"Frank was a nasty person. Not a psychopath. Not a brainwashed cult member. Not possessed by the devil. Just a thoroughly rotten individual, focused on his own gain and very entitled." A shiver ran through me, remembering my personal encounter with him. "I feel as though I need a shower just talking about him. Should Mrs. Wainwright bear some responsibility for the way he turned out? I don't know. He was her only child, and she loved him."

"Why isn't she here?" Alice asked.

"She's dead," I said.

"We didn't hear about that!" Emily said.

"The police kept it very quiet. As their next of kin, you're being informed now."

George cleared his throat.

I'd gone a bit off script there, but I was caught up in the drama. "Are you familiar with Medea? I know Dani is. Rather than let her children be slaughtered by the king's men—remember the legend? The king banished them along with her. Or let them grow up with Jason, her ex-lover, to become spoiled and vain. There are several versions. So, she killed them out of love to save them."

"What does that have to do with anything?" Phil snapped.

"It was when George was proposing that I realized that Frank's murder was an act of love. I suspect she'd fooled herself about his nature for quite a while, but when he used her to try to get the guardianship, she had a feeling her life might be cut short as soon as she was in position. Then he could reveal that she was his mother and step into her shoes."

"But why did he kill Gen?" Alice asked.

"Because Gen figured out what both Tina and Frank were doing and confronted them. That sealed her fate. She cared about Frank, who thought there was a fortune hidden at the Estate, and she loved you, Tina."

"How did he know something was hidden at the mansion?" Alice asked.

"Working for Gen gave Frank access to the private estate papers," Tina said.

"Frank used Gen in several different ways," I said.

Alice nodded.

Tina spoke up. "A treasure was referred to many times. People searched for it, but no one could find it. None of the clues panned out. One was that the secret 'lies with the cat.' So, Adrian and I dug up the pet cemetery. Nothing."

"That explains the vandalism," Mina said quietly. "I'm afraid I used Cass to find the location of the treasure. But it wasn't the kind of fortune you, Adrian, and Frank were looking for." Mina held up the diary. "It was this."

Adrian was shocked out of his careful pose. "An old book?"

"It's a diary, a record of the estate and the people and animals that lived there. It's a priceless treasure."

"Not in my opinion. Not worth killing or dying for," Adrian said.

Mina put the diary down.

"I think Mrs. Wainwright was ill," I said. "She was pale and fragile and couldn't die knowing that Frank would go on killing for the inheritance and anything else he wanted. Once she was established as guardian, she would no longer be useful to him. He could step in as an inheritor at any point thereafter. She realized that he'd been using her his whole life to provide for him, get him out of scrapes, and do his bidding. He didn't love her as his mother. But she loved him." I turned to Dani. "He went down a side trail to delay getting help for you, Dani. He meant you to die on that hike. His mother caught up to him as he walked along that cliff over the rocks and pool below. She accused him of attempting to murder you. They argued, according to the other two hikers on a hill above them. He called her a senile old bat. She shoved him. He grabbed for her to save himself, and she just leaned into him and they both went over. She killed him before he could kill her. She killed him out of love. This whole guardian competition reminds me of a tontine, and it's been just as deadly."

Adrian stood. "You proved that Tina and I had nothing to do with the murders."

I shook my head. "You really are going to try to brazen it out, aren't you? After everything you and Tina have done?" I turned to George. "Can I say take them away?"

Epilogue

Jack, Gillian, George, Dani, and I sat to eat at three on Sunday afternoon at the dining room table with candles and fresh flowers.

"Thanks for being here this early. You'll notice that you each have a can and a glass in addition to your water glass. The distillery wanted us to try their latest creation, so give us some feedback, and I'll let them know how you liked it when I provide them with the finished Coastal Ghost Hop page, which was CaRiMia's most recent job. Check it out. You might want to join us for the event. Jack and Gillian are going to come back for it."

We all poured our cider.

"A toast to new beginnings."

We raised our glasses and then drank.

"It's been quite a while since Jack and I have had a mid-afternoon Sunday dinner, but that's the custom we grew up with. Then we'd have a late supper to tide us over until the next morning. This isn't nearly as fancy a meal as our mother put out with the cut glass crystal bowls."

"And gherkins," Jack said.

"That, too. Jack and Gillian will still hit traffic going home, but the earlier the hour, the easier it'll be. Jack, will you start the noodles? Dani, can you get the garlic bread going?"

"Happy to now that I'm pretty sure I won't be arrested for anything." She picked up the bread basket, took a slice, and passed it to me.

George reached into his pocket and held up his keys, which were dangling from a pair of mini-handcuffs.

"George! No bread for you!" I passed it back to Dani.

"Kidding." He stuffed his keys back in his pocket and reached across the table for the bread.

Dani held it away from him for a moment and then passed it.

"Seriously, George," Gillian said. "Is everything tied up with a ribbon? It appears that Alice and Emily like each other enough to become close friends over the ordeal and co-administer the trust. Both love cats. Why were you questioning them? Did you think they bumped Frank off at the park?"

"I needed eyewitness confirmation of information we'd gotten from the hikers."

"But they said it was an accident."

"Their accounts dovetailed nicely with all the other accounts we've gathered. What was throwing us off was an early assumption that both murders were committed by the same person instead of two people. When we discovered some earlier murders that Frank had committed to narrow down the field, we figured out that there were two of them and that they weren't working together. Dani is a descendant, as you know, and that's the main reason she was a suspect, but she would have had a better chance with Gen alive. Frank's death on the hike really threw us."

"Glad to be off the suspect list," Dani said,

sprinkling parmesan on her spaghetti.

George helped himself to salad. "We'll be busy for a bit getting the paperwork done."

"Speaking of paperwork." I took the salad bowl from George. "Genevieve Genealogy has closed, and CaRiMia has lost the contract, but Mina suggested that the trust, Alice, and Emily hire us to do a website with the history of the trust, including a section about the murders, which I predict will be very popular. Happily, Ricardo's already taken a lot of the photos that we'll need. They decided to open the mansion up for tours and even want to do a ghost walk handled by the local paranormal group."

"You watch. There'll be a gift shop, too." Dani took the salad bowl from me. "I can hardly wait to see how you portray the murderous Wainwright clan. Which name is it really? Wright or Wainwright?"

"Please pass the Vidalia onion dressing. Thanks," George said. "From what we've been able to ascertain, the family name is Wainwright."

I took the dressing from him when he finished. "According to Gen's notes, he was a great admirer of Frank Lloyd Wright and changed his name."

"There's no legal name change."

I set the dressing down. "No. I think it was a smoke screen. After he saw to it that his mother was chosen, by process of elimination—literally—if nothing else, he would have stepped forward as her son at some point in the future. She would probably have gone into decline from the cancer, or he would have arranged an accident or perhaps it would appear that she'd taken her own life. Any way he managed it, he would have become the guardian, which would have left him free to hunt for the treasure."

"His mother had cancer, and he knew about it, of course," George said.

"But to kill your child…" Gillian shook her head. "I can't imagine."

I leaned forward. "And speaking of DNA, genealogy, and children, if you and Jack don't hurry up, our line may die out altogether. I'm afraid our branch of the family is rather overeducated and undersexed."

"Speak for yourself." Jack took another swig of his India pale ale.

Gillian smiled. "Oh, I don't think you have to worry on that score." She pulled out a sonogram. "Twins."

Jack spit beer.

A word about the author…

I currently live in Cape May County in New Jersey after spending years in the San Francisco Bay Area with my Maine Coon cats Sierra and Ginger.

I attended Clarion Writers Workshop for Science Fiction and Fantasy at Michigan State University and sold a story I wrote there to Damon Knight for The Clarion Awards anthology. I wrote technical manuals in Silicon Valley and also published several poems and science articles as well as a couple of chapters in Research & Professional Resources in Children's Literature: Piecing a Patchwork Quilt.

I've also taught English in high school and community colleges.

****

https://www.renaleith.com

****

If you enjoyed this story, leaving a review at your favorite book retailer or reader website would be much appreciated. Thank you!